"Don't expect the Germans to be anything but brutal and murderous. They will try to exterminate us because they must! Resistance in any form—no matter how small—is a deadly threat to the Nazis.

"Charles Marceau, should you decide to join us and should you get caught, the Germans will not consider what you've done as childish pranks. Be assured that your age won't save you. At the best, a Nazi concentration camp. At the worst, a firing squad. . . ."

MILTON DANK, who served in France during World War II, is the author of two nonfiction books on this period, *The French Against the French* and *The Glider Gang*. A graduate of the University of Pennsylvania with a Ph.D. in physics, Dr. Dank lives with his wife and two daughters in Wyncote, Pennsylvania.

THE LAUREL-LEAF LIBRARY brings together under a single imprint outstanding works of fiction and nonfiction particularly suitable for young adult readers, both in and out of the classroom. The series is under the editorship of Charles F. Reasoner, Professor of Elementary Education, New York University.

The Dangerous Game

Milton Dank

A LAUREL-LEAF LIBRARY BOOK
Published by
Dell Publishing Co., Inc.
1 Dag Hammarskjold Plaza
New York, New York 10017

Copyright © 1977 by Milton Dank

Laurel-Leaf Library ® TM 766734,
Dell Publishing Co., Inc.

ISBN: 0-440-91765-4

Reprinted by arrangement with J. B. Lippincott Company

Printed in the United States of America

First Laurel-Leaf Library printing—January 1980

TO NAOMI,
GLORIA,
AND JOAN

MAKE READY THE CHAINS:
FOR THE LAND IS FULL
OF BLOODY CRIMES
AND THE CITY IS FULL
OF VIOLENCE.

 EZEKIEL 7:23

1

"Who's there?"

A powerful flashlight beam swept both sides of the deserted street, pausing only to penetrate the blackness of the doorways. Startled by the light, a hungry dog fled from an overturned garbage can into a nearby air raid shelter.

Huddled on the floor at the back of the shelter, the boy held his breath as the frightened dog hurtled over him. Now they could not fail to spot him! Never had he felt so naked and exposed, but it was the helplessness of his situation—he was unable to run or hide or fight—that brought unaccustomed tears of frustration to his eyes.

Charles had heard the German patrol just before they'd entered the street. In the conquered city, after curfew, the pounding of hobnailed boots on the pavement could only mean the enemy. In his haste to hide himself in the shelter, he had stumbled over an empty gasoline can and had fallen heavily to the concrete floor. The loud metallic clanging of the can bouncing off a wooden bench had sounded like a shellburst. Halfway up the narrow street, the German patrol had frozen in their tracks.

The entrance to the shelter leaped into sharp white relief as the light paused menacingly on it. Trembling, Charles buried his head in his arms and waited. His knee throbbed from the fall.

The German sergeant lowered his submachine gun and clicked off the flashlight. "Just a damned dog knocking over a garbage can," he said. "Let's go." Behind him the patrol rose, shouldered their rifles, and resumed their march down the street. As they passed the boxlike shelter, one of them idly shone his torch through the door, but he did not bother to peer inside. After all, it was only a dog. . . .

When the sound of their boots vanished in the distance, Charles waited for two minutes, then got up slowly and brushed the dirt from his clothes. Not too far away, the famished dog growled a warning, but Charles whispered soothingly and the threatening sound stopped. By now, his fear had given way to anger. He had almost been caught out after curfew by a German patrol—and all because of Lynx. Where was he?

The young worker with the crooked smile and slanted eyes had set this place and time for the rendezvous. The hour was too close to curfew and therefore dangerous, but the man whom they were to meet could not travel openly during the day. Now it occurred to Charles that this might have been a scheme to get rid of him. Had his insistence on wanting to help aroused Lynx's suspicion? Rather than receiving a curt refusal, was he to be left alone on an empty street to be picked up by the first passing patrol? Was the young mechanic really part of a Resistance network, and

did he intend to take Charles to meet the leader?
Where was he now?

It was a hot July night without a trace of a
breeze, and under his thin jacket, Charles was
bathed in sweat. Somewhere in the gloom beyond
the square, a clock struck the quarter hour. The
two loud notes rattled down the street and
startled the boy hidden in the shadows. Aware
that panic was beginning to grip him, Charles
concentrated on evaluating the situation. Minutes
passed as he struggled to reach a decision. The
more he thought about it, the sillier it seemed to
stand there and wait to be arrested. Better to give
up this attempt, return to the apartment, and try
again later.

Suddenly he was aware of another presence in
the deep gloom of the shelter. There had been no
sound even from the dog, only a deeper darkness
behind him, and then the whisper of breathing.
There was no apology, no explanation—just orders
in the familiar rasping voice. "We will cross the
street and walk slowly towards the square. Stay
close to the buildings and don't get too far ahead
of me. I'll tell you when to stop."

It was in front of a small entryway next to a
printing shop, with a window sign that proudly
proclaimed that it specialized in birth, engage-
ment, and wedding announcements, that Charles
felt a restraining hand on his shoulder. The
shadow behind him moved towards the door and
scratched softly three times. There was a short
wait, and then the door seemed to open by itself
and Lynx pushed Charles inside. With the none-
too-gentle guiding hand on his shoulder, Charles

was propelled in the darkness down what seemed to be a narrow corridor and through a door at the far end. The room in which he found himself seemed to be large, but it was hard to be certain. Only the sound of their footsteps echoing off the walls gave him any sense of its size.

There was a blaze of light as Lynx turned on a desk lamp. He pointed to the chair in front of the desk, and then disappeared into the darkness behind it. Charles heard the scraping of a chair, but the lamplight did not reach into the corners of the room. Strain his eyes as he might, he could see nothing beyond the desk top. With a resigned sigh, he sat back, folded his hands on his lap, and waited.

The room was silent except for the squeaking of the chair when Lynx shifted his weight. Charles tried to control his anxiety, but he sensed that the two of them were not alone, that someone else in the room was watching him closely, looking for a sign of nervousness or fear. *Perhaps this is the way they do it in the Resistance,* Charles thought; *certainly they have to be sure of their recruits. Why don't they begin?*

As the nerve-wracking silence continued, broken only by the creak of the chair, he began to wonder if it had all been a bad mistake. So many things had happened so quickly.

Only four weeks ago, Charles had been sitting in his comfortable apartment writing to his mother. He had written the letter in the long sloping hand that his schoolmasters had praised, pausing now and then to listen to the sounds of confusion in the streets below. It had been the be-

12

ginning of the hot spell, and the windows overlooking the rue Copernic had been wide open to
catch any vagrant breeze.

Sitting erect behind the large desk, he com-
posed the letter carefully, occasionally running
his fingers through his black hair. He was a handsome boy, tall for his sixteen years. His American
mother had given him an oval face with light blue
eyes and a full sensuous mouth, now tight with
concentration. From his French father and a long
line of soldier ancestors, he had inherited a muscular body as well as discipline and an old-fashioned sense of honor. In the closely knit family,
the parents had jokingly called their only son *le
Beau Sabreur*, "the Handsome Cavalier."

While he wrote, he chewed thoughtfully on his
lower lip; as usual, Charles Marceau was meticu-
lous when writing in English. There was little
chance that his mother would ever read his
words, but he phrased the letter carefully anyway. Although his father had been wounded—how
badly he did not know; his mother had gone to
Belgium to be with him, but Charles had not
heard from her—the boy tried not to appear
gloomy. It was difficult, almost impossible. In the
middle of June, 1940, Paris was dying.

"Yesterday," he wrote, "the school was closed,
since most of the students have left with their
families for the south. The streets are filled with
rumors of the approaching German armies and
nothing has been done to calm the people. The
government swore to defend Paris to the last, then
fled to safety after declaring it an open city. In

the newspapers there are only blank columns where the censors have cut out the truth, but one learns a great deal by reading between the lines of the official communiqués. Sunday, 'Our gallant troops inflicted a terrible defeat on the enemy at Montdidier, stopping the timid German advance dead in its tracks. The enemy has failed everywhere.' There was even some mention of a second Miracle of the Marne. Monday, 'Our heroic army fought brilliantly in the face of great odds in the suburbs of Compiègne'—fifty-six kilometers closer to Paris! Such duplicity is hard to believe."

Charles paused, biting the end of the old-fashioned steel-nibbed pen pensively. It was allowable to criticize the government (both his parents detested the weak politicians who had kowtowed to Hitler until the last moment), but the French army was a different matter. He remembered his grandfather, a colonel in the regular army, who had led his regiment through the butchery of 1914–1918 and who had always spoken so softly and reverently of the bravery of his soldiers. Two years before, in the little chapel at St. Étienne, they had buried him, still stern, still uncompromising, surrounded by the regimental flags and his weeping men. *No*, Charles thought, *my father will be hurt if I go on in this vein.*

"There is no doubt that our soldiers have fought bravely against superior numbers and arms," he continued, "and one need never be ashamed of the French army. Yet the fact is that the Germans will be in Paris tomorrow, or the day after at the latest.

"I have decided that I do not want to see them

marching in triumph through *my* streets, perhaps even under *my* window. So, I shall leave."

It was difficult to imagine the Germans in Paris. M. Chailland, the principal of Charles' school, had sobbed when he had announced to the awed students that they must leave their classes and await the arrival of the enemy. Charles had half expected him to write *"Vive la France"* in a bold hand on the blackboard as the Germans broke into the classroom. The students had been solemn but secretly delighted at the unexpected holiday. It was hard to grasp the reality of the defeat, but the escape from Latin compositions, endless readings of literary works, and the strict discipline of the masters—that was real enough.

As Charles tried to concentrate, the noise from the street below increased, and he walked over to the large casement windows and closed them.

"It is unbelievable, Maman," he wrote, "the scene in the streets. The cry is 'Every man for himself,' and terror is the spur. They are fleeing in anything that moves: cars, trucks, taxis, bicycles, even baby carriages and wheelbarrows. I saw M. Durand, the baker, pack his wife, his three children, and his two assistants into a delivery van filled with furniture. He had strapped some mattresses on the top as protection against enemy planes and did not neglect to take along those two horrible poodles that I have detested for so long. Mme. Durand was weeping, which frightened the children and made her husband so furious that he swore at the poor assistants as if *they* were responsible for losing the war. It appears that the entire neighborhood is gone now, crowding the roads south towards the Loire and undoubtedly doing a great deal of harm to our soldiers trying to reach the front."

He paused guiltily and reread the last sentence. Would not he himself be contributing to the traffic jam on the roads?

"I shall leave Paris by way of St. Germain—the trains still run that far. By going due west, I shall avoid the crowds fleeing to the south. There is a bus that goes to Evreux, although I am not certain that it still makes the trip. If not, I will walk. If I keep off the main roads, I should have no problem in getting to Cherbourg and Aunt Liselle. Please do not worry about me. I am strong and the hunting and fishing trips with Papa have fitted me for even this journey.

"The key to the apartment will be in the concierge's room—she left hurriedly the day before yesterday with her cat, muttering something about a sick friend in Deauville. She was very pale and dressed all in black as though going to a funeral. A very funny sight indeed, weaving through the mob on that old bicycle with her cat sitting in the front basket and spitting at everyone who came close. The last I saw of her, she was disputing the turn at the corner with an overloaded cart pulled by a scrawny piebald horse.

"André Moisson—you remember, Maman, the boy in my class who is so in love with you—left Paris yesterday. His father, the pharmacist with the big store on the rue Lauriston, was killed during the German attack at Sedan. It was very sad, and everyone at school made a big fuss over André. M. Chailland delivered a little speech complete with references to 'died for his country' and including 'on the field of honor'! André spoke to me of finding a boat for England or North Africa to continue the war. It is all very brave and reckless—'revenge for my father,' that sort of business—but I don't think that what we will need to finally beat the Germans is sixteen-year-old tank drivers."

A dull, distant roar rattled the windows and made the crystal pendants of the chandelier tinkle melodiously. Somewhere beyond the Bois de Boulogne, across the Seine, a thick black pall, licked at the base by fiery tongues, was already climbing into the cloudless sky.

"Well, there it is, dear Maman. The city is to be turned over to the enemy. They have blown up the fuel depots as Poissy and provided a shroud of black smoke for a dying city. You can see why I cannot remain, although it shames me to think of mingling with a panicky mob.

"I trust that by the time you receive this letter, Papa will have recovered from his wound. I send you both a big kiss and will await word from you at Aunt Liselle's. Your loving son, Charles."

He sealed the envelope carefully and addressed it to Mme. Claire Marceau, Hôpital Militaire, Wavre, Belgique. Uncertain of the correct postage, he affixed two ordinary French stamps. Then, propping the letter in front of him, he leaned back in the high-backed chair and stared at it pensively. Had he said it all? Was it perhaps too alarmist? Poor Maman, would he be adding to the sorrows she undoubtedly already had, Papa wounded and her son cut off in a Paris soon to fall

17

to the enemy? Still, it would be a comfort to her to know that he was on his way to safety in Normandy.

Charles shrugged his shoulders. It was unlikely that the letter would ever reach Wavre or even that his parents were still there. But if it should—and they were—well, any sort of news would be less frightening than none at all.

His knapsack was waiting in the hallway where he had put it after packing the night before. For the trip, which he knew would be arduous—and more than a little dangerous—he had selected a few articles with great care so that excessive weight would not tire him: an extra shirt, two pairs of heavy socks (necessary for walking even in the heat of summer), the foot powder recommended by his father during one of their hunting trips, a road map with the proposed route outlined in red, a ground sheet to keep off the damp while sleeping out of doors, a lightweight undershirt and shorts, a pocket knife, some fishhooks and about twenty meters of line, two cans of meat paste, and a long loaf of bread cut in half and wrapped in waxed paper. He had thought of adding his father's Webley revolver, but had quickly decided against it; he knew how to use a gun, but this one was too heavy. If he were stopped by the Germans, a gun would only mean trouble. Better to play the lost innocent and use his wits to get out of any unfortunate encounter.

Mentally he checked off the list of the items, reaching into the knapsack and touching each in turn. He was thorough in all things, a trait that delighted his father but often exasperated his im-

patient mother because of the time he would take
to be certain that everything was in order. When
he finished the count, he looked at his wristwatch:
1422 (he preferred the military time system,
which avoided the possibility of confusing A.M.
and P.M.), or 2:22 PP.M. It was time to go.

The gas jets in the kitchen were off. Charles
carefully unscrewed all the fuses in the electrical
box at the back of the hallway closet, placing
them on top of the box where they would be eas-
ily spotted when his parents returned. The
revolver he shoved deep inside a stuffed toy bear
that he had discarded ten years ago, but that his
mother insisted on keeping on her dresser. As
much as he loved his dear Maman, there were
times when her sentimentality and lack of logic
betrayed her American background. Not, Charles
hastily assured himself, that he was less proud of
his Pennsylvania ancestors, who had brought civ-
ilization to the wilderness of the Monongahela,
than he was of the Captain Lucien Marceau who
had fought in the Napoleonic wars and had died
in the retreat from Moscow. It was simply a matter of perspective.

Knapsack slung over his shoulder, Charles
paused for a moment in the doorway, looking
back at the apartment so cluttered with lovely
and expensive things: the fans, vases, screens, and
little ivory animals that his mother loved and that
he and his father tolerated for love of her. They
had been very happy here on the rue Copernic.
His father's duties at the War Ministry had sel-
dom interfered with the round of parties, picnics,
and motor tours of the countryside that, before

the war, had been the prerogative of the young couples who were the Marceaus' friends. Charles had never felt left out, for when his parents had returned from an afternoon at Auteuil or Fontainebleau, they had always awakened him and regaled him with stories about the wonderful sights they had seen and about how a certain major had fallen into the fountain. Laughter, peals and peals of laughter—that was what he remembered most.

He left the apartment key in the concierge's room on the ground floor, hanging it carefully on the wall with the others. M. Crémieux, the aging jeweler who entertained young girls so frequently in his ornate apartment on the fourth floor, was gone, as were the Dumaires, who shared the third floor with the Marceaus. Their keys had not been touched for the last three days, and an ambitious spider had already covered them with an almost invisible web. Charles was amused to see that the concierge had hidden her mattress and bedding, but had left the door unlocked.

In the street, the mournful parade of fleeing people rolled on, hastened by the ominous pall of smoke in the distance. Charles was reminded of the colored illustrations in his copy of *The Last Days of Pompeii* showing the fat Roman senators and their wives fleeing before the fiery rain of ashes. But now the inhabitants of this upper-middle-class district were mingled with the workers and clerks of the neighboring streets. Cars were moving slowly through the bottleneck of bicycles and carts, all piled high with children, pets, bedding, and furniture—the cherished possessions of impoverished households. Charles weaved his way through the overwrought, shouting mob and climbed the street towards the subway station.

At the corner of the rue Lauriston, two sweaty policemen were angrily scrubbing away some graffiti smeared with whitewash on the brick wall of a small hotel. They had evidently just started, for Charles was able to make out the message: PARIS RESTE FRANÇAIS—Paris remains French. Across the narrow street, a young man—seventeen, eighteen?—dressed like a factory worker was watching the two gendarmes with a twisted grin on his lips. His eyes caught Charles' and held them for a moment. Then his right hand came out of the pocket of his dirty windbreaker and, turning his body to hide the gesture from the police, he made the obscene gesture that marks extreme contempt in all Latin countries. His rigid finger still pointing at the pavement, the young man walked slowly down the rue Lauriston, his shoulders hunched derisively.

For me? Charles wondered. *For the policemen? Or perhaps for the Germans and for all Frenchmen who let them in?* "Paris remains French." M. Chailland and the other masters would have approved of that sentiment—short, patriotic, logical. And even if Paris did remain French, what of the rest of France—the north already overrun by the enemy divisions and the south crowded with homeless wanderers? *No*, Charles thought, *the proper expression at this time is "France remains French"!* Paris, as Papa had often reminded him, was not France. It was only the capital; it was not

21

Normandy, it was not Provence, it was neither Alsace nor Lorraine.

Still, that young worker, uneducated and probably ignorant of the greatness of his country's history, had been able to take a stand (Charles never doubted that it was he who had smeared the words on the wall), while the others—the aristocrats and the bourgeoisie—fled. Could one pay tribute to duty with one's feet?

For the first time in his life, Charles Marceau was deeply ashamed. His father and the other soldiers did their duty without question, even in defeat, while this young mechanic in his dirty jacket acted only by instinct and from the purest sense of patriotism. Yet he, Charles Marceau, the son of an army officer, a boy whose ancestors had fought bravely on a hundred European battlefields and in the dark forests of Pennsylvania—he was about to flee. His father had often talked to him quietly but firmly about duty and honor, and now he was about to betray both.

Red with shame, Charles turned on his heel and ran back to the apartment. On the way, he tore up the letter and scattered the pieces in the gutter. Someday soon, he would have to write another letter.

Two days later the Germans entered the empty city in triumph. Rank after rank of gray-green-uniformed troops marched in a victory parade down the Champ-Élysées, their bands blaring at the head. Huge Nazi flags hung from the Eiffel Tower and the Chamber of Deputies to mark the conquest, and Charles trembled with anger at the sight of the swastika—that crooked black spider on a red background—that now floated above his beloved city. It was more than a patriot could stand; he had to do something. But what could one sixteen-year-old boy do against the mighty German Wehrmacht?

It took Charles over three weeks of the most painstaking searching to find the young workman again. Every morning he arose early and walked through the neighborhood, peering into the little bars and the few shops that were still open. He bought a street map of Paris and carefully marked the areas he had covered. Gradually he expanded the search, always looking for whitewashed slogans on the walls or other signs of resistance. Night after night he returned discouraged to the apartment, but in the morning he was up early, map in hand, to try once more.

A week after Paris fell, the old Marshal, Philippe Pétain, a hero of the First World War, tearfully announced on the radio that the war was lost and that the enemy had been asked for an armistice. Stunned, Charles listened to the quavering voice begging the Germans for mercy. He could not believe it—a Marshal of France crying!

Eager to invade England, Adolf Hitler quickly granted the armistice, but the conditions were humiliating. The agreement was to be signed in the same railway coach and at the same spot where Germany had surrendered in 1918. France was to be split into two and occupied by the Germans north of the demarcation line, including Paris. The rest of France was to be governed by the Marshal, whose new capital was to be the resort town of Vichy. Two million French soldiers were to remain in German prison camps until England was defeated, and France was to pay 400 million francs a day for the privilege of being occupied by the victorious troops of the Third German Reich.

The old Marshal bowed his head and signed, and Charles Marceau continued his search for those who said "no" to the armistice and the occupation.

After almost a month without a clue, he was about to give up when he spotted the young worker in the back of a cheap bar on the Left Bank, joking with a pretty waitress. Charles waited until the girl left, then sat down opposite the young man he had sought for so long.

His heart pounding with excitement, Charles started the conversation with a description of the scene on the street corner—the policemen scrubbing off the patriotic inscription and Charles' feeling that it was his duty to stay in Paris and fight the invaders. He pleaded feverishly for five minutes while the young worker listened expressionless; then he stopped, exhausted, his throat and mouth dry from arguing.

Lynx—it was the only name he gave—denied at first that he had any contact with a Resistance group. It took Charles over an hour of pleading—and quite a few drinks—before he was taken seriously. Very reluctantly, Lynx admitted that he might know someone "who does something against the Nazis." He could make no promises, but if Charles wanted to talk to this man . . . After another drink, a rendezvous was set for three days later in the air raid shelter behind the National Library.

Charles returned home light-headed but triumphant. He had succeeded in contacting the Resistance. A big decision had been made. It was a beginning.

Only five minutes had passed, according to Charles' watch, but it seemed like hours. Squirming in his chair, he was about to protest the delay when a scar-faced man limped slowly out of the darkness and sat down at the desk.

2

The man was rather short and very thin, with a pale, bony face riddled by burn scars, and a high forehead. The light from the desk reflected from cold gray eyes that watched Charles unceasingly. Charles sat up straighter in his chair, unable to take his eyes from the man behind the desk. This was not a man to play games with; this was a man accustomed to command and to be obeyed.

There were no polite preliminaries, no introductions. It would have been unthinkable for the interrogator to offer his hand. When he spoke, his voice was soft and educated; not once did he raise it, and yet Charles detected a hint of steel underneath.

"Your name?"

"Marceau, Charles." He gave his name in the inverted order he would have used naturally if the question had come from a schoolmaster—or a policeman.

"Age?"

"Sixteen—" there was a moment's hesitation—"in three months."

The questioner nodded thoughtfully, as if he appreciated the accuracy of the response.

"Where do you live?"

"Seventeen rue Copernic, third floor."

"I know the neighborhood. My congratulations. It is very fashionable." There was a slight emphasis on the last word.

Charles flushed. "We are not rich. My father is an army officer, and that's not the best-paid job in the world. The apartment was bought with a small inheritance my mother received from her father."

The man behind the desk began to doodle on a large yellow pad. Charles forced himself not to look down. He fixed his gaze on the interrogator's blue silk tie, sprinkled with what looked like white anchors. Where had he seen that insignia before?

"So your father is in the army? Where is he now?"

"I don't know. He was wounded fighting in Belgium shortly after the start of the German attack. My mother went to be with him and I have had no word of either of them since. Perhaps they were evacuated at Dunkirk and are now in England."

"And you've been alone in Paris all this time? How do you live?"

"I am still in our apartment, and a friend of my father's at the bank has been advancing me money from our account. I had thought of going to stay with my aunt in Normandy, but it is impossible to travel. Besides, I've been hoping that my parents would write to me here, but so far there has been nothing."

A thousand times Charles had pictured the

bombs ripping through the military hospital or his parents' ship sinking in the Channel. *They may be dead*, he thought sadly. *They may never know what I am doing.* He saw the interrogator blink and shake his head slowly. *He understands. He heard the pain in my words.*

"Why do you want to fight the Germans?" the scar-faced man asked. The cold edge was gone from his voice and he sounded almost matter-of-fact.

"This defeat . . . this occupation." Charles' voice broke from anger. "It makes me ashamed."

"Yes, the Nazis have that gift. They make men ashamed and willing to fight just to get rid of that sense of dishonor. In the end, Germany will lose the war because men and women cannot live ashamed of themselves and their country. Do you believe that?"

Charles nodded vigorously.

"Good. By the way, I am called Vidal—never mind my real name, it is of no concern in this war. Be prepared to lose your own name if you decide to join this army of shadows." Vidal paused reflectively, wrote Charles' name on the pad, and then drew a line under it.

"What we do nowadays is trivial and yet terribly important. The people are still crushed by the defeat; we must help them to rise again. They think the Germans are invincible; we must show them that this is not true—has never been true. They have lost faith in France; we must restore that faith, that belief in *la Patrie*. If need be, we must do this by the sacrifice of our lives."

Charles shivered and gripped the arms of his

chair. The man behind the desk might have been giving a lecture to a favorite student, so bland and professorial was his tone, but the powerful words overwhelmed the boy.

"A spark must be struck," Vidal continued, "one strong enough to light a fire that will arouse all of France and burn the Germans off our soil. Our first duty is to keep the feeble flame of resistance alive. We are only a small group, and to the Germans insignificant, but not for long. Soon they will turn and we will be at their backs; then the real war—our war—will begin."

There was a long pause, and Charles heard a chair scrape loudly in the background. "In every war there are casualties. Don't expect the Germans to be anything but brutal and murderous. They will try to exterminate us because they must! Resistance in any form—no matter how small—is a deadly threat to the Nazis. They will react with cunning, deception, and treachery. We must be on our guard every second. You, Charles Marceau, should you decide to join us, will be given certain tasks, such as writing slogans on the walls or distributing our newspaper. They will seem trivial and even useless to you, but if you should be caught, the Germans will not consider what you have done as childish pranks. Be assured that your age won't save you. At the best, a Nazi concentration camp. At the worst, a firing squad. So, think carefully before you answer this next question. Are you prepared to work with us, knowing all the risks and dangers? Will you accept the orders of your superiors without question, doing quickly what must be done? Are you ready to lie, cheat, and, if necessary, kill so that France may live again?"

Charles swallowed hard under the intense, icy gaze. "Yes, to all your questions."

The thin man shook his head sadly. "I had almost hoped that you would refuse. You're very young. But we are so few, and when there are no men to fight for our country, we must use boys. You will stay here tonight; there are beds on the top floor. Tomorrow we will begin your instruction."

He rose and leaned over the desk to grip Charles' hand solemnly. *Like a benediction,* Charles thought wonderingly, *a laying-on of hands—as if I had been admitted to a religious order.*

There was a loud click and the desk lamp went out. "We must give you a name," the solemn voice said out of the darkness. "Forget your own. From now on it will only be a danger to you and to your family. We will call you *Faucon*—Falcon. Does that suit you?"

Falcon—yes, that pleased Charles very much.

The "classes" were held in the storeroom above the printing shop, a long, narrow, dusty room with a low ceiling. Scattered about were bales of old posters, uncut book sheets, long-discarded type frames, and smelly cans of ink. The one small window was nailed shut and its glass covered with black paper against inquisitive neighbors. The room was stifling in the July heat.

A heavyset old man was standing at the blackboard, and there were three others in the room.

When he first entered, Charles noted them carefully. A woman of about forty, prematurely gray and rather carelessly dressed, was smoking a cigarette and talking in an undertone to a husky young man in a summer suit who kept smiling emptily and nodding his head. Standing by the door and staring at nothing in particular was a girl of about eighteen wearing an attractive white dress. Her face was rather pretty, although her nose was a little long, and there was something about her—the defiant way she stood or the way she carried herself so erect—that attracted Charles. *A salesgirl in one of the more fashionable stores,* he decided, *and afraid . . . as we all are.*

Again there were no introductions—"You already know too much about each other," the old man in the shabby black suit grumbled. The class began as soon as they were assembled. It started with a grim warning that stunned the four novices. "Experience has shown," the old man said, "that the first three months are the most dangerous for the new recruit. If at the end of that time you have escaped being arrested, either because of luck or because you learned your lessons well, you will enter the second most dangerous period. Then you will start to think that you are too smart for the Fritzes. You will start to take little shortcuts—nothing serious at first: late for a rendezvous, maybe just two or three minutes; a password wrong or even forgotten in your haste to get the job done—all these will begin to add up, and one day, poof! A hand on your shoulder, the final words 'German police!' and goodbye."

The old man hawked and spat into a large red

handkerchief, watching their reactions closely. Charles saw the girl in the white dress stiffen. The gray-haired woman crossed herself hastily. "That won't help you," the instructor warned.

"If you last a year, the odds will start to turn in your favor. You'll have learned all the tricks, all the little lies that protect you. By then you'll have become valuable to us, trained, disciplined, maybe even important. If you are arrested, we'll try to help you. It may not be possible, but we'll try. Until then, you are nothing to us, and if the Germans get you, we will risk nothing for you. This may seem hard, but this is a hard business, and the mission comes first. While the group exists, the struggle goes on . . . no matter who falls. In any war there are casualties, so pay attention and maybe, just possibly, you'll last."

Grumbling and shaking his head as if doubtful that they could make it, the old man strutted to the blackboard and began the first lesson: the organization of the Resistance.

Old Kléber was a veteran of Verdun who had won the Military Medal for bravery during the 1914–1918 war. A lifelong socialist, he had fought in Spain against the Fascists and had been one of the last to cross the border back into France when the Republican government had fallen. He was an expert on propaganda and sabotage, and delighted in telling long, often boring, stories of his feats behind Franco's lines. Still, he was the only one in the group with any experience in clandestine work, and he was listened to with great respect.

For the next four months, the routine was the

same. The four novices met in the storeroom and listened to Kléber—Charles wondered why he had picked the name of one of Napoleon's generals as his *nom de guerre*—talk on the organization of the German armed forces, the operations of the Nazi police (particularly the Gestapo), and the purposes of the underground struggle. "Our main victory consists not in propaganda or in collecting intelligence, as vital as they may be, but simply in existing. We are too feeble to be a real threat, but as long as one Resistance man or woman is alive and working, the Fritzes can never rest easy on our soil!"

There were talks on codes and passwords, on how to arrange a rendezvous: "Crowded streets and subway stations are the best." Kléber gave lengthy advice on how to approach a stranger: "Ask for directions or a light for your cigarette; look for a bulge in his coat pocket or under his armpit. The Gestapo don't like to go around unarmed. Paris makes them nervous. They lost too many soldiers trying to get here in the last war." The old veteran paused to glare at his listeners as if blaming them for the defeat and the occupation. *He's not wrong,* Charles thought. *Our fathers beat the Germans in 1918 at the cost of a million dead, but we let them into France, and now two million French soldiers are in Nazi prison camps.*

"The Gestapo like to make arrests between three and five in the morning. That way the prisoner is half asleep, startled, and unable to get his story straight. Always have an escape route planned. If someone knocks on your door at those hours, get the hell out the back or through a window onto the roof, and run to a 'safe house.' Don't wait to see if it is the concierge complaining about the curtains not being drawn for the blackout. One night it won't be."

Note-taking was strictly forbidden—"We're not planning to publish these lectures"—and Charles wondered if the others were absorbing the mass of information any better than he was. After all, he had been a top student, but this was not at all like memorizing the verses of Victor Hugo or the dates of the French kings. Uniforms, unit badges, armies, divisions, the ranks of the dreaded S.S., arms and explosives ("We don't have any yet," Kléber complained), methods of sabotaging German vehicles using household materials—"Put sugar in the fuel tanks; it gums up the carburetors something fierce"—this and more was all presented in an ever-increasing flood. Charles' head reeled with the pain of memorizing. And always there was the grim warning: "Learn or die!"

One day, Charles boldly sat next to the attractive girl they called *la Mouette*—Seagull. *The name suits her, he thought. She always seems to be scanning some distant horizon.* His attempts at conversation were utter failures. The girl stared at him coldly once, then turned away. Charles was so annoyed he almost failed to hear old Kléber's words, the stinging, blunt warning that he would at first refuse to believe.

"You think that all Frenchmen and Frenchwomen are allied in this fight against the invaders? You are wrong. Disabuse yourself of that belief or it may kill you. Ninety-five percent of them blindly follow the old Marshal down the path of collaboration, risking nothing and hoping to get through this mess with a whole skin and enough to keep themselves and their families fed and warm. They'll sit on the fence until they see who will win this bloody war, and then they'll fall off onto the winning side. If they can do so without endangering themselves, they won't betray you—after all you might turn out to be the winner, although they don't think so now—but they won't help you either. Not if the German police are after you. Of the remaining five percent, only a handful are fighting the Germans as we are . . . the others are traitors and your deadliest enemies. They are the eyes and ears of the Gestapo. In fact, that's what we call them—'the French Gestapo.' They'll cut your throat in a minute to please their new masters!

"At first," the old man continued, "it was the dregs of the underworld—thieves, swindlers, pimps, and prostitutes—who had been recruited or had offered their services to the Nazis. But now, with everyone hungry, cold, and scared, the weak, the brutal, the sadistic, the psychological misfits who cannot find the strength to believe in France swell the ranks of the pursuers and the torturers. Beware of them. Be suspicious of everyone outside of this group. You have no friends besides your comrades in the struggle. Someone is not an ally because he speaks French."

"Nor," Charles turned and whispered into the girl's ear, "is someone a friend just because *she* speaks French." Seagull did not answer, but Charles thought he saw a slight change in the

35

thin line of her lips. He could almost swear that she was smiling.

Week after week, they sat for long hours in the classroom, listening to the bitter truths that other Resistance men and women had died to uncover and pass on. Autumn came and brought welcome relief from the heat. The leaves changed color and soon began to fall. Vidal, sniffing the breeze like a sailor, predicted an early winter and a bitter one.

For his sixteenth birthday, October 17, Charles invited Seagull to dinner: "A can of sardines and a loaf of yesterday's bread." She declined politely but firmly. Charles spent the evening alone in the cold apartment practicing Morse code.

By the beginning of November, the classroom was freezing, and a cherry red potbellied stove could not keep them warm. There were some angry words as the four novices showed the strain of the hard work and the enforced isolation. As a test and to relieve tension, Kléber decided to send them out, singly and in teams, to carry out assignments—"Your homework, except that you'll do it in the streets." Charles rode the subway, sticking pamphlets between the seats and the walls of the cars, where they were certain to be seen by the curious. Walking through the railroad stations, he would unobtrusively drop pamphlets on the benches or in the stalls in the men's rooms. Friendly newspaper vendors would turn their backs while he planted the pamphlets between the pages of the most popular newspapers, taking special delight in stuffing the copies of notorious collaborationist sheets.

That winter was the worst in fifty years. The

Seine froze and the coal barges could not reach the city. The people shivered, wrapped paper underneath their coats, and haunted the post offices, where there was still heat. Charles elbowed his way through the crowds, dropping folded pamphlets discreetly into coat pockets, shopping bags, even umbrellas.

And Paris was shabby. There were no new clothes in the stores and no cloth with which to make them. People resoled their shoes with wood, for leather had been gobbled up by the insatiable German war machine. Soon food became scarce, and even with ration coupons and after a long wait in the queue, there would often be nothing left to buy. There was constant grumbling about the old Marshal's weakness in the face of the Germans' looting of the necessities of life, but Charles sensed that this was only talk. The Parisians were still not ready to risk anything in the struggle against the invaders.

"It will take a bigger shock than missing a meal or two," he told Kléber. "It will take something like . . ." He hesitated, unable to continue the thought.

"Like the shooting of hostages," the old man finished. "You must learn to say the words, Falcon. It is part of your education."

Charles arrived five minutes early to relieve Porcupine. Remembering that such appointments must be kept exactly on time—neither too early nor too late—he walked into the bookstore on the corner and looked casually over the collection of best-sellers on the front table. Noting with disgust that they were all the works of prominent collaborators, he forced himself to glance through three of them. *My God,* he thought, *have we sunk so low that we allow Hitler to be praised in public as the savior of Europe?*

Promptly at a quarter to five, he left the bookstore and sauntered into the rue Lauriston. "Remember," Kléber had drummed into his pupils, "you must be inconspicuous at all times. Never call attention to yourself by your actions, your manner, or even your dress. An ordinary citizen going about your daily routine, that's what you are, and you must act the role every second of every day." The old man would get so excited during his lecture that he would begin to sputter and stammer. "You are in a diving suit at the bottom of a deep hostile sea, under tremendous pressure. Lose your 'cover'—arouse suspicion—that is the same as ripping open your diving suit! The German ocean will do the rest."

Porcupine was sitting at a table next to the front window of the café, moodily staring at a glass of wine. He did not look up as Charles entered and sat at the table in front of him. *They've named him well,* Charles thought: *prickly, ready to bristle, and none too sociable.* He took the newspaper from his jacket pocket and was soon absorbed in the story of student demonstrations the day before—Armistice Day; there had been shooting by the Germans. Out of the corner of his eye, he saw Porcupine yawn, rise from the table, put on a rather worn military overcoat, and leave.

The watch had been changed. Now Charles was on duty.

The orders that Vidal had given Charles were perfectly simple. There was a café called the Normandy across from Number 93 rue Lauriston. At exactly 4:45 in the afternoon, Charles was to relieve Porcupine there. Vidal, too, had stressed the importance of being exactly on time. "If you are early, that makes two of you we will lose if the police get suspicious. If you are late, Porcupine will assume you have been arrested and will leave immediately, and no one will be covering the house." Charles was to stay at a table watching the entrance to Number 93 until 6:00. He was to memorize the descriptions of everyone who entered or left, and was to report this information to Vidal at the printing shop after he was relieved.

No sooner had Porcupine disappeared than a man came around the corner and walked hurriedly into Number 93. Short, fat, small, deep-set eyes in a round fleshy face. Piggy, Charles named him silently to himself, and then repeated the name to impress it on his memory. He shut his eyes for a moment and pictured the stranger crossing the street to see if he had forgotten anything important—oh yes, the briefcase. The man had carried a black leather briefcase.

Charles had always been proud of his memory, but it seemed stupid not to make notes on his observations. When he had suggested this to Kléber, the old veteran had almost screamed his disapproval. "Write nothing down, do you hear, nothing! If you are arrested and searched, they'll know immediately. What kind of schoolboy keeps lists like that?" But suppose thirty, forty, or even fifty people went in and out of the house across the street?

No one had told him why the gray stone building with its arched windows and curved balcony was so important. Neither Vidal nor Kléber had offered an explanation, and by now Charles was too disciplined a member of the group to ask. The first rule of clandestine work, it had been repeatedly impressed upon him, was to accept orders without question. One would be told only what was necessary to successfully carry out the mission. More than that was a danger to the underground agent and to the group.

A black Peugeot automobile stopped in front of Number 93. A young man—five-ten or eleven, muscular, with a square, ugly face topped with a mop of blond hair—got out from behind the wheel, glanced carefully up and down the street, and then entered the building. Blondie: gray suit, white shirt, and a totally inappropriate tie, Charles ordered into his memory. He prided himself on his knowledge of good tailoring.

Business was slow after Blondie. Charles sat relaxed at the table, pretending to be absorbed in the sports page. Twice the bored waiter took his order for "A glass of Chablis—no ice, please—and one of the better vintages, if you have it." Muttering under his breath, the waiter had sullenly brought him a glass of cheap white wine. Charles caught something about "snotty kids these days" and blushed at the thought that he had made himself conspicuous. If someone were to inquire, the waiter would remember him.

At five minutes to six, a woman stepped out of the gloomy entrance into the light. Charles glanced up casually from the sports page and picked up his glass of wine. Over the top of the glass, he saw her clearly: about thirty-five, dark complexion, fashionably thin, modishly dressed— only the Germans' friends could afford to dress that well—jet black hair. Even while Charles was cataloging the woman as Mata Hari, Blondie came running down the steps, grabbed her by the arm, and hustled her into the black Peugeot. As they drove off, he could see them quarreling in the front seat.

Thoughtfully, Charles stared at his drink. Expensive clothes could have been bought before the war, but one did not drive a car today in Paris without gas coupons, and these only came from the Germans. To get them, one had to give the enemy something that they wanted. Even doctors and essential municipal employees got around on bicycles or in the rickety *gazogènes* that burned green wood and coal as fuel.

Friends of the Germans, collaborators eager to fit France as a vassal into Hitler's New Europe. Traitors out of political belief, or just greedy little people unable to join in the common suffering.

Traitors. Kléber was right.

A German staff car stopped in front of Number 93. A man got out, spoke briefly to the driver, and then walked up the steps. Tall, balding, a sallow face with a prominent hooked nose and a brutal

expression. Charles recognized him instantly:
Henri Lafont, the ex-convict, one of the leaders of
the French Gestapo in Paris. Now he knew why
he was watching the building; it was the lair of
the cruelest band of killers that the Nazis had
ever recruited to hunt down the Resistance. There
could be no mistake. Lafont's picture had been in
the newspapers frequently, showing him mingling
with his German masters at the racetrack and at-
tending official functions at Gestapo headquarters
on the avenue Foch.

Five fifty-seven, Charles noted automatically.
Henri Lafont—"Roman Nose," the frightened Parisians called him—entered the building.

At exactly six o'clock, a young man in a gray
mackinaw came into the café. Charles waited
several minutes, then folded his newspaper,
picked up his bill, and walked to the cashier. Behind the counter, the surly waiter checked the
bill, took the money, and spread the change on
the small tray. As Charles leaned forward to pick
it up, the waiter whispered, "It does not pay to be
too concerned with that house over there, young
man." Flushing with embarrassment, Charles left
quickly.

When he turned the corner, Blondie was waiting for him. The black Peugeot was at the curb,
the dark woman slouching behind the wheel. *In
case I went in the other direction,* Charles
thought.

The grip on his arm was painful. "Since you're
so interested in our home, let's go take a look," the
blond man said with a tight smile. He pushed
Charles ahead of him, never relaxing his grip. The

woman backed up the car, turned, and followed them.

It was 6:04 P.M., Charles noted bitterly. Blondie and Mata Hari reentered the building—with one stupid amateur in tow.

3

The first blow was the worst because it was unexpected. Seated in a chair, his hands manacled behind his back, Charles had been examining the office carefully, noting the steel bars and shutters on the two windows, the huge cabinet sheeted with metal plates, and the submachine gun casually lying on one of the files. Blondie was standing behind him, his hands still gripping his shoulders, while Lafont sat on the edge of the desk, smoking and asking the questions. When Charles hesitated for a moment, Blondie smashed a palm quickly against his cheek. It was so sudden that Charles felt the tears welling up in his eyes from the pain, but he bit his lip and concentrated on the interrogator.

"Don't try to lie to us," Lafont said. He spoke in a weird falsetto, incongruous in such a dangerous man. "It is useless and it will only go harder with you. Who told you to watch this building? For whom are you working?"

"Watching? But I assure you, sir, that I was not—" Charles' denial was interrupted by another brutal slap. This time Blondie hit him across the mouth. Charles could taste the blood flowing from his lower lip.

Lafont sighed and puffed his cigarette. "Why be difficult, young man? Your friends can't help you now, and wouldn't if they could. They've crossed you off the list. Why suffer all this when all you have to do is tell us a few names?"

"But, M. Lafont, I was only—"

"You know me?" Lafont said. It was clear that he was flattered by the recognition.

Charles nodded vigorously. "Everyone in Paris knows Henri Lafont," he said politely. "They say you are the most powerful man in the whole Seine department, that even the Germans take orders from you."

It was all true, Charles thought bitterly. This ex-convict, liberated from a French prison by an air raid, had hastened to put himself and his gang in the service of the Gestapo. Now they ruled the streets, murdering and stealing, tracking down Resistance members, Jews, and Communists, and helping the Nazis to loot France through phony "purchasing bureaus" that bought up scarce materials for the German war machine. Protected by their German police cards, supplied with guns and cars by their masters, they were the scourge of the occupied. Even the French police feared them and dared not interfere.

Seeing Lafont preening himself at the flattery, Charles hastened to press his advantage. "Surely, M. Henri, no one would be foolish enough to risk your displeasure. Why would I want to keep track of your movements? Do I look like a terrorist?"

Lafont examined Charles carefully. Then he

looked questioningly at Blondie, who shook his head furiously.

"Why were you in the Café Normandy?" Lafont asked. He leaned forward and placed the tip of his cigarette close to Charles' face.

Rigid with fright, Charles watched the burning tip move slowly closer and closer to his cheek. He was pressed back against the chair, held immobile by the rough hands gripping his shoulders. "I was waiting for a girl!" he screamed.

The red tip paused a millimeter from the skin and there was a low sizzling sound and the pungent odor of burning hair. Then Lafont leaned back, a broad smile on his face, and flicked the cigarette ash into an ashtray. "Go on," he said.

"She works as a maid for the Charpentiers— André Charpentier is a school friend of mine. I study there almost every day. She is very pretty, very nice . . . I asked her to have a drink with me at the Normandy . . . it's her day off. She said yes, and I thought . . ."

"I can imagine what you thought." Lafont howled with laughter. "How old is this love of yours?"

"Nineteen, twenty."

"Ah, an older woman. You should be ashamed of yourself, chasing skirts when you should be worrying about irregular verbs and Molière. What will your parents think?"

Charles felt Blondie's hands relax their grip on his shoulders. He played the embarrassed juvenile perfectly, a tremor in his voice, downcast eyes, even pleading for sympathy and understanding. "My father vanished, fighting with the army in

Belgium. My mother went to find him. I haven't heard from either of them since."

There was a long silence as Lafont lit another cigarette, walked thoughtfully around the desk, and sat down. He stared at Charles through a cloud of bluish smoke as if unable to make up his mind. Charles could hear Blondie breathing heavily behind him. When Lafont asked the inevitable next question, he was ready.

"What does this girl look like?"

Rapidly, Charles described Seagull, putting in a few extravagant touches as a love-smitten teenager might. "Tall—for a girl, that is—brunette, lovely white skin and a perfect mouth. Her nose is a trifle long, but it fits her face marvelously. High cheekbones that give her the look of a Tartar princess, and her voice—"

"My congratulations, Marceau," Lafont interjected dryly. "Well, where is this beauty of yours? Why has she stood you up?"

Charles shrugged his shoulders as best he could with his wrists pinioned behind him. "Perhaps she could not get away. The Charpentiers are very demanding, very strict."

"More likely she found someone a little older and a little better heeled than a sixteen-year-old schoolboy," Lafont jeered.

This time the embarrassment was real. This was exactly what Charles had been telling himself for the last month. Every time he had tried to talk to Seagull, the idea that she might laugh had frozen him. But to hear it from this traitor with his girlish voice . . . Lafont watched the flush cover Charles' face and grinned maliciously.

"Louis, show our young friend the cellar. I have some business affairs to attend to, so bring him back in fifteen minutes and we'll decide then." With a nonchalant wave, Lafont dismissed them and turned to the papers on his desk.

Blondie dragged and shoved Charles to the cellar, which had been rebuilt since the Gestapo had commandeered the house from its American owner. Four cells had been constructed, each with a heavy wooden door, and the whole cellar painted a stark white. There was a strong odor of disinfectant, and Charles was reminded of a hospital corridor where the patients had to be locked away. A sullen-looking guard in shirtsleeves sat behind a table near the entryway, a submachine gun across his lap. He nodded casually to Blondie, then went back to his study of the racing form.

There was a judas—a small hole covered by a swinging disc—in each door. Blondie pushed Charles to the nearest cell, opened the peephole, and, grabbing his hair, brutally forced his face against it. "Look, then, since you were so anxious to see this."

For a moment the pain from his mouth and cheek blurred Charles' vision. When it cleared he could see into the semidarkness of the cell: a straw mattress and a crumpled blanket on the floor, a bucket in the corner, a barred window high on the far wall through which filtered a solitary beam of light. At first the cell seemed empty, but as his eyes became accustomed to the gloom, Charles saw the man.

It would have been hard to recognize it as human even if the bare bulb that dangled from the damp ceiling had been lit. More like a gray-white plaster dummy tied to a chair, its head slumped on its chest, naked. There were long red slashes all over its body, and a low whistling sound of pain came from its lips. The cell was filled with a fetid odor that even the disinfectant could not disguise. Under the whippings, the prisoner had lost control of his body functions.

Charles gagged and twisted away from the peephole despite the painful grip on his hair. The guard and Blondie laughed as he struggled to get away from the door, afraid that he was about to disgrace himself by being sick.

"Well now," Blondie sneered. "The young gentleman has no stomach for the entertainment we provide here." He pushed Charles against the wall, half lifting him off his feet. "Listen carefully, Marceau. Keep up these lies and that will be you in there, bleeding like that. And when we are done with you and you've told us everything we want to know—and you will, for here no one is silent very long—we'll hand you over to our German friends on the avenue Foch, who will hurry you in front of a firing squad!"

The guard waved his submachine gun. "Why wait, Engel?"

Fighting nausea, Charles stumbled out of the cellar and up the long flight of steps to Lafont's office. Fear had paralyzed him. He believed every word of Blondie's threats. Nothing that Kléber had taught him had prepared him for this horrible sight. They would torture him, and sooner or later he would talk.

Lafont was conversing with a well-dressed

older man who sat primly in front of the desk, a briefcase on his lap. Neither looked up as Charles was pushed into the room and onto the sofa. Clearly their negotiations had been successfully concluded.

"Agreed, my dear Lasserre," Lafont said. "Ten thousand chamois skins equal in quality to this sample, to be delivered to the depot at Abbeville by the twenty-second. Don't fail me, now. The Boches are sticklers for punctuality."

The businessman rose and shook the ex-convict's hand enthusiastically. "A pleasure doing business with you, M. Henri. One avoids all the fuss and red tape of trying to sell in the regular channels."

Lafont eyed Lasserre with thinly disguised contempt. "And avoids the government taxes plus the shame of having to deal with the Nazis directly. To say nothing of the danger if the Resistance should find out."

Lasserre flushed and started to protest, but Lafont had lost interest and waved him out. The businessman glanced nervously at Charles, then hurried to the door. *I wonder what he makes of me,* Charles thought wearily. *One doesn't usually find a teenager with a bloody mouth and his hands manacled behind his back in a well-run business office. And that poor devil down in the cellar—does he ever hear him scream?*

Lafont finished signing the papers with a sigh of satisfaction, lit a cigarette, and stared thoughtfully at the ceiling. "Our young friend has now seen what happens to those who oppose us?" Blondie grinned and nodded. "Very good. It is all a matter of education, not all of which can be obtained in even the best schools today. By the way, Louis, did that Jew talk?"

"Not a word, boss."

"Too bad." There was genuine regret in Lafont's voice, as if he had suffered a personal loss. "I would have liked to present the whole group to our German friends. Such a coup would have raised our standing immensely with those fellows on the avenue Foch. Still, one must be satisfied at times with minor successes. Let's not waste any more time on that pig—he might die on us. Call Sturmbannführer Vogtler at Gestapo headquarters and have him pick up what's left of that brave Resistance leader."

Lafont penned a notation in a large ledger. *Has he entered my name in that book?* Charles wondered.

Slamming shut the ledger, Lafont leaned back in his chair and stared moodily at Charles.

"You may go, Marceau," Lafont said suddenly. Blondie's protest was cut short by a cold stare.

Charles stared unbelieving at the large-nosed man behind the desk. For a moment he did not trust his ears. Had Lafont really said that he could leave, or was this just a taunt before sending him back to that terrible cellar? He struggled to raise himself from the sofa, still looking questioningly at the "boss."

Lafont smiled thinly and pointed at the door. "Sorry about all this, but you have only yourself to blame. These are not the days for foolish actions—not even by schoolboys."

Blondie unlocked the handcuffs and pushed

Charles towards the door. Wild with relief, he mumbled his thanks. Lafont cut him short with a wave of the hand. Then as Charles opened the door—

"Marceau!"

Startled, Charles turned. "Yes, M. Henri?"

"The next time you set a rendezvous, use another part of Paris." There was no mistaking the menace in the icy tone. Charles nodded dumbly and fled. In front of the building, the astonished chamois dealer paused before entering his car to watch the boy sprint across the street.

It was only after Charles had turned the corner and was out of sight that he stopped and leaned limply against a lamp post. Fear, humiliation, and disgrace flooded over him as he fought for control. The tears were a relief, and soon his body shook with racking sobs. Then he was violently sick.

It was almost eight o'clock when he entered the apartment. He locked the door and pulled the curtains over the windows before turning on the lights. In the bathroom, he examined his face in the mirror. It was a shocking sight; a large blue-black bruise on his right cheek and the caked blood on his lip frightened him. He washed his face carefully in cold water and rubbed some of his mother's eau de cologne on his forehead. Then he drank a little brandy to get rid of the foul taste in his mouth and stretched out on his bed. Drained of all strength, he fell asleep.

The insistent ringing of the telephone awakened him with a start at around midnight. Sleepily, he reached for the receiver and mumbled "Hello." There was no answer, just a menacing silence, then a click as someone hung up. Charles stared at the receiver for a moment, then returned it to its cradle. Was it one of Lafont's men checking on his address? Or one of the group finding out if he had returned home? No doubt his relief at the Normandy had reported his capture and his unexplained release more than an hour later. *They must be wondering what happened in between,* Charles thought. *Still, I obeyed orders.*

He remembered Kléber's instructions: "If they nab you, if you are taken in a sudden roundup for identity-card check, or if for any reason you are questioned by the Gestapo or the police and are released, don't come back here! You are certain to be followed. Go home and wait for us to get in touch with you. We will do this when we are sure it is safe. Remember, we don't know what went on between you and the enemy. We must assume that you are a danger to us, and if you come back here, either you are stupid—criminally stupid—or you have been 'turned' and are working for the other side. In either case, you are a deadly plague that we must get rid of—and the Resistance has no jails in which you can be safely kept until the war is over."

Charles went to the window and checked the dark street below. It took him a while, but finally he spotted a man in the dark doorway of the pharmacy across the street. It was after curfew, so the watcher could only be someone with a permit to be out after hours, say a German police card.

Old Kléber had been right again. It would have been fatal to return to the printing shop.

In his parents' bedroom, Charles checked the window that led to the fire escape. From the top of the fire escape, Charles could reach the roof, cross to the roof of the next house, and so on until he reached the cross street at the end of the rue Copernic. A quick descent on the fire escape there and Charles could lose himself in a dozen small streets crowded with shops and apartment buildings. This was his escape route.

Suddenly, he found that he was hungry. There was some cheese and a croissant in the refrigerator, and he poured himself a large glass of milk. The larder was nearly empty and he scribbled a note to remind himself to shop tomorrow—or rather today. He took his feast on a tray into the dining room, sat at the large table, and began to eat. He was ravenous. It was hard to believe that one could still feel hunger after a visit with the Gestapo.

For the next few days, Charles made a great display of leading a very ordinary life. He slept late, had a leisurely breakfast, did his morning exercises, then went shopping. More and more foods were disappearing from the counters of the grocery stores and butcher shops. Rationing had been started by the old Marshal's government, but the amount of meat, butter, and even vegetables that could be bought with the coupons was being cut almost weekly. Charles stood in the long lines in front of the stores, listening to the complaints of the housewives who had been waiting for hours for the meager foodstuffs with which they were expected to feed their large families. He was regarded with suspicion, and muttered comments were made. With almost two million men in the German prisoner-of-war camps, it was rare to see a young man not in school or working in some factory making goods for the Nazis.

All this time, he was aware that *they* were watching him. He knew most of the neighbors and the usual habitués of the little café on the corner, so it was no problem to spot the strangers, the one who lounged so idly by the newspaper stand, or the dwarfish Gestapo agent in a loud checked overcoat who dawdled over his drink at an outside table despite the bitter cold.

In the afternoon, Charles would walk along the crowded boulevards, looking at the few goods still left in the shop windows. From the first day of the occupation, the Nazis had bought everything in sight with the money paid by Vichy as a war indemnity. Like a swarm of locusts they had descended on the shops and had carried off all the fine goods for which Paris was famous, and which had vanished long ago from a Germany geared to war production. Now the shelves were empty, and the Parisians were struggling to live amid ever-mounting shortages of the most basic goods. For a pair of leather heels for their shoes or a darning needle, they had to find the black market and pay the exorbitant prices demanded by profiteers, who grew fat on their miseries.

After a meager supper, Charles read or listened to music on the radio. The hourly news programs were filled with Nazi boasts of "devastating air raids on England . . . London is in flames again as our gallant pilots . . ." This had been going on for months and it was obvious that the British were still holding out. Looking at a map, Charles decided that the Germans would have to look elsewhere for a means of reducing Britain: cut the lifeline to the Empire, perhaps—the Mediterranean, Malta, the Suez Canal. He played the game of German moves and British countermoves for hours, just as once he had moved regiments of tin soldiers across the living-room floor. Except that now—after the rue Lauriston—he knew what it meant when those brightly painted little soldiers fell over under the casual annihilating wave of his hand. Even the red of the uniforms had a different meaning.

As hard as he might try, he could not keep his mind from dwelling on that horrible experience. The pain came back at the most unexpected times. It was like poking at an abscessed tooth with his tongue; he could not stop himself. He was deeply ashamed of the fear he had felt, grateful for his escape, and just a little proud of his ingenious story. True, the Charpentiers' maid was a redhead and none too pretty, but the name was a very common one and impossible to trace. All in all, it had been very clever, quick thinking on his part. But he knew that the next time he would not be so lucky, and, remembering the man in the cellar, he shivered.

A week after it started, the surveillance ceased. The strange faces disappeared from the rue Copernic and, although Charles watched carefully, no new ones appeared. Had Lafont decided he was not worth the effort? Charles checked the reflections in the shop windows as he walked, but there were no suspicious movements in the crowds behind him. He stood on a corner for five minutes, then turned suddenly and went back down the street, but no one turned to follow. That night, he used the last of the coffee to celebrate the lifting of the shadow. He was free.

As the days passed with no indication that he was being trailed, he waited impatiently for a telephone call from Kléber. He felt alone, isolated, cut off from his friends. It did not seem fair that he should still be under suspicion. He had taken that terrible beating and had kept his mouth shut. He had obeyed orders to the letter and had not endangered the group. Why didn't the damn phone ring?

A month had gone by since his arrest, a long boring month during which Charles had grown more and more morose and had become oppressed by a sense of his comrades' ingratitude. "You are nothing to us . . . we will risk nothing for you"—Kléber's words came back to him again and again. Still, it was very hard; he had never felt so alone in his life.

He was sitting in the Tuileries garden watching the workmen putting up the Christmas decorations when Seagull walked down the path and sat down on the bench next to him. She did it very prettily, hesitating for a moment and glancing about for another place to sit. Luckily the only other bench in sight was filled by a young mother and her three chattering children admiring the banners, tinsel, and lanterns. Charles saw that she was wearing a thin cloth coat and felt sorry for her; it was bitter cold. They sat side by side for a while, ignoring each other and watching the passersby to see if anyone was paying undue attention to them.

"Hello, Falcon," the girl finally said softly. Charles grunted and stared down at his shoes. His sense of having been badly treated had not left him. Seagull glanced at him briefly.

"You understand," she said. "We had to be certain of you."

"If I had talked or if they had 'turned' me, you would all be in prison by now." There was a sullen, angry tone in Charles' voice. He kicked a pebble across the path.

"Even you do not know *all* of us. You couldn't have given them names and addresses because you don't know them. A raid on the printing shop might catch a few, but most would escape. The only sure way would be for them to let you go and . . ."

The sentence was left dangling, but Charles knew what she meant. The girl adjusted the scarf about her neck and continued, "Kléber and the others are very proud of you."

Charles felt the anger drain from him at this unexpected compliment. "And you?" he asked.

The girl turned and looked at him boldly. The cold air had brought a faint flush to her cheeks and her hazel eyes seem to sparkle. Her smile warmed him.

"If it is important, I think you were splendid."

Well now, Charles thought, *that's more like it.*

58

He lowered his eyes and gave a deprecating wave of the hand as if his bravery was not worth mentioning. In a low, serious voice, he reported on his experiences, stressing Lafont's questions and his own cover story. He underplayed the beatings and the cigarette, but when he told of the man in the cellar, he choked and he had to stop to get a grip on himself. The girl waited, never taking her eyes off him.

"Tell Kléber that ten thousand chamois skins are being delivered to the Fritzes at Abbeville on the twenty-second. They were sold by a man named Lasserre—short, stocky fellow of about forty, big ears, drives a blue Renault, license number TR 6519. I think London will appreciate that information."

The girl nodded. "I remember Kléber telling us why chamois skins are important. The Germans use them to filter out dirt when they fuel their planes. Ten thousand skins at Abbeville means a large German air fleet will be moving into that area soon. Yes, the R.A.F. *would* like to know that."

Charles explained the layout of the Gestapo headquarters, mentioning the barred windows, the armored cabinet, and the other precautions against a sudden attack. There were two guards with submachine guns inside the main entrance and one on duty in the cellar. He could not tell how many of the Gestapo were in the building, but he had heard a lot of noises in the corridor and on the stairs. Somewhere between fifteen and twenty, he would guess. And Blondie's name was Louis Engel.

Seagull listened attentively. When he was done, she complimented him quietly on the wealth of detail. "It's amazing that you can remember so much after going through a time like that."

Charles admitted that the details had only come to him later, when he was safely back in the apartment. Before that, the whole thing had been a mixture of pain and terror. Then, yielding to the loneliness of the past month, he said soberly, "Tell Kléber that I want to come back."

Seagull rose from the bench and offered her hand. He took it gently, marveling at the softness of her skin. The girl started to leave, then turned, leaned towards him, and whispered, "You might at least have made me a student at the Sorbonne or a rich bourgeois' daughter, but a housemaid!" The amused glint in her eyes belied the mock outrage in her voice.

Charles grinned happily, then spread his hands, palms up, in appeal. "At my age, one does not have too many choices. Remember, it had to be believable!"

She walked down the wintry path, erect as ever. Charles watched her until she reached the crossing. There she stopped, turned briefly, her hair blowing in a sudden gust, and waved to him. Then she was gone.

His heart pounding, Charles stared at the crossing long after she had disappeared. Only later did it occur to him that if one of Lafont's men had been watching, he would have reported that the pretty housemaid had finally kept a rendezvous.

4

Two days before Christmas, ominous black-and-red posters blossomed on the walls of Paris. Later they were to become all too familiar, but these were the first, so curious crowds gathered to read them. The text was in two languages, German on the left and French on the right, and it was signed at the bottom by the German military commander. Charles had to read it twice before the meaning sank in: "The engineer Jacques Bonsergent, of Paris, was condemned to death by a German military tribunal for an act of violence against a member of the German army. He was shot this morning."

When Charles arrived at the printing shop, Vidal was correcting proofs in the back room. His scarred face was unusually pale. When he looked up and saw Charles stuffing copies of the one-sheet newspaper into his overcoat pockets, he called him over. "You saw the posters?" Vidal asked.

Charles nodded. He had been upset at first, especially with all the women crying around him, but now he accepted the fact. He had always known that sooner or later the Germans would start shooting people. As Kléber had said, accepting the inevitability of executions was part of his education in underground work. Why was Vidal so broken up about this one man?

"Did you know Bonsergent?" Charles asked.

Vidal nodded. "So did you. Bonsergent was Porcupine."

His voice was so low that Charles did not hear the name at first. Then he remembered the big, heavy fellow in the army overcoat whom he had relieved at the Café Normandy the day he had been arrested. The gloomy unsociable type . . . so it had been Porcupine.

"What happened?" Charles demanded.

"Something almost banal. Bonsergent was walking with his girl when a drunken German soldier stumbled into him. They both tumbled to the ground and the Fritz started yelling that he had been attacked. Bonsergent smashed him in the face and began running but was collared by a patrol. They found out that his papers were false. He wouldn't tell them who he was so they condemned him for attacking the Fritz." Vidal went back to his proofreading, muttering something under his breath. All Charles could hear was the word "fate . . . fate . . ." repeated over and over.

In the classroom, Kléber was waiting for him. They pulled their chairs to the potbellied stove and warmed themselves while they talked. Since he had rejoined the group a week before, Charles, under the old man's direction, had been searching Paris for a new German navy headquarters that was supposed to be located in Neuilly. So far, he had been unsuccessful, but today he had spotted a staff car with a navy driver in front of a café. Unfortunately, he had been unable to, follow the car with his bicycle. Kléber memorized the address of the café. "Maybe the driver eats there or has a girl friend who works there. Next time we'll have a truck nearby to follow him."

Charles unbuttoned his coat and savored the warmth from the stove. There was snow on the ground and he was in no hurry to get back on the streets. Drowsily he slumped in the chair and closed his eyes. Kléber saw that his fists were clenched and that there was a twitch at the corner of his mouth.

"What's bothering you?" the old man asked.

Without opening his eyes, Charles answered, "Bonsergent."

Kléber hawked and spat on the red-hot stove. "He shouldn't have run. The Fritz was clearly drunk and the girl could always have said that the soldier had insulted her. As long as there was no identity check, Porcupine was all right. But the idiot ran."

Did they torture him, Charles wondered, *to make him talk? In another dirty cellar somewhere? And when they tied him to the execution stake, did they offer him a cigarette and a blindfold as they do in the movies? Did Porcupine smoke?*

"*La Mouette!*" Kléber's harsh voice broke into Charles' reverie. He opened his eyes and stared at the wizened old man, who was looking furiously at the stove. He waited for Kléber to continue.

Obviously the old socialist was reluctant to discuss the matter. Finally, he choked out the words.

"She has been coming to your apartment three or four times a week."

How did they know? Charles wondered. Was he being watched? Did they still think that his release by Lafont was too easy, that his scars were too few? He could feel the anger in his throat again.

"You may think that your private life is your own, Falcon, but that is nonsense. We depend too much on one another. There can be nothing hidden from your comrades in the fight. Suppose it turned out that you were a secret tippler and had a loose tongue when drunk. Or that your mistress had a cousin in the *Milice* that she was fond of—"

"She's not my mistress," Charles said hotly. "And you know she has no relatives in the *Milice* or any other Vichy police gang. She is a comrade and she came at first to collect the information I had gathered. She was the only one who bothered. As far as the rest of you were concerned, I could have rotted in that apartment."

Kléber listened patiently.

"You've been back for a week now. Make your reports to us." The old man leaned forward and patted Charles' knee affectionately. "Don't you see what the two of you are getting into? You are both now more vulnerable than ever. If one of you is taken, the other is in terrible danger. Besides, worrying about each other every minute of the day will make you careless. You'll forget the job to be done, the mission to be carried out. All you will think about is whether the other is safe . . ."

The old man's voice trailed off. Talking about

such things made him uncomfortable, Charles guessed.

No more was said, but the girl's visits ceased abruptly, leaving Charles as resentful and lonely as before. Seagull gave him no reason and never mentioned if Kléber had spoken to her. When they met in the printing shop, often to pile up the newspapers for distribution, she was friendly, but once again distant. For a moment in his apartment, as they had sat on the floor in front of the fireplace, Charles had felt a closeness, an intimacy that he had known before only with his mother. Now it was gone, another sacrifice made for the struggle. When Lynx asked certain suggestive questions about their evenings together, Charles cut him off with a cold stare. He was aware of the hungry looks that the young worker cast after Seagull and put it all down to jealousy. That made him feel good.

Shortly after the New Year, the postal system started to function again and there was a long-delayed letter from his Aunt Liselle. She was worried about Charles. No, she had had no news of his parents and only one postcard from his cousin Pierre in a camp near Stuttgart. Pierre said that there were rumors that the French prisoners of war were to be released. The Germans were taking all the food and even the farm animals from the Cherbourg area—paying with "occupation money," of course, but that brought less and less every month. Could he come and visit her? She was lonely and Charles was her only relative, etc., etc.

He threw the letter away. He was sorry for

Aunt Liselle and for her worries, but travel now was out of the question. More and more both Kléber and Vidal looked to him for the important work of the group. They were still so few and there was so much to be done.

He would have to admit that he was very tired. The constant strain of clandestine work was wearing all of them down. Tempers were short, and only yesterday Raven had almost gotten into a fight with Lynx. They had been separated before they had come to blows, but Charles knew that frayed tempers were one of the prices they were paying for eternal vigilance. *Sooner or later,* he thought, *one of us will make a blunder out of sheer fatigue and the Germans will nab us. No one helps us. At best, the vast majority of our fellow countrymen are neutral in the struggle. At worst, they are on the Nazis' side.*

Slowly the terrible winter passed. By the middle of March, the snow was gone, but even as the cold released its grip, the Germans tightened their hold on the city. Rations were cut almost every week. By spring, every Parisian was living on a weekly allowance of five pounds of bread, three pounds of potatoes, and a few stringy vegetables. Meat—when it was available in the butcher shops—was limited to twelve ounces per week. Those who still had something valuable to trade bought food at inflated prices on the black market. The poor and those trying to live on small pensions were starving.

Vidal ordered fake ration cards printed and distributed to the needy. When the Nazis started to arrest and deport Jews to concentration camps, false identity cards were fabricated to allow the persecuted to flee to the unoccupied zone. Although the new suffering brought a few recruits to the group, the work load was crushing.

On June 22, 1941, came the stunning news that Hitler had sent his armies into the Soviet Union. At first there was jubilation, and Lynx, a Communist militant, proudly predicted an early German defeat, but the Russian armies crumbled on all fronts and the morale of the Resistance—despite Vidal's efforts—sank to a new low. As the Nazis went from one victory to another, apathy and resignation flooded the group. Quarrels broke out over tactics. What good were the few copies of the newspaper that they distributed at such a great risk? What help were the pamphlets that people just threw away unread? Would forged ration cards and identification papers stop the German armies? With great patience, Vidal explained that since the group was small and unarmed, it had no other choice.

Two months after the German attack on the Soviet Union, Charles returned to the apartment and found a note that had been slipped under the door. On a cheap sheet of lined paper were typed the words "Barbès—Clignancourt side—Wednesday, 0800." There was no signature. *Tomorrow is Wednesday,* Charles thought, *and the Barbès subway station is a long way off. I had better get up early.*

The Barbès-Rochechouart subway station was in a working-class district behind the railroad station called the Gare du Nord. To get there,

Charles took the eastbound subway at the Victor Hugo station. Barbès was one of the stops on this line, about halfway to the terminal. As he left the train and headed towards the steps that led to the platform of the Porte-de-Clignancourt line, Charles paused to tie his shoelace. This allowed him to see if anyone behind him had stopped abruptly. No one had, so it was safe to assume he was not being followed.

On the Clignancourt platform, the rush-hour crowd waited patiently for the train. They were mostly factory workers and salesgirls, with a smattering of government clerks and heavy laborers. There were even a few German soldiers in the mob waiting to be taken to the military offices of the occupation authorities. There was nothing unusual in this scene. In Paris in August, 1941, the occupied and the enemy had accepted the sullen truce, and studiously ignored each other's presence.

A train rattled into the station, stopped with a long whining sigh. Its doors opened to accept the mob that flooded the second-class cars. Only the Fritzes traveled in the single first-class car; patriotic Parisians avoided sharing the trip with them even if it meant jamming themselves into the overcrowded second class. When the train closed its doors and pulled away from the station, Charles saw that the platform was empty except for himself and the ticket collector at the far end, who was watching him curiously. He looked at his watch: two minutes to eight.

The automatic door at the entrance that kept the reckless from diving onto the train at the last moment opened and a new crowd of travelers soon packed the platform. Charles scrutinized their faces as they came through the narrow entryway, but none was familiar. It was all beginning to look like a practical joke in very bad taste. Then he saw them, and his heart began to pound violently.

They came through the barrier late, as if to be certain that it would close soon behind them. The first two were strangers to Charles; muscular young men dressed in windbreakers and tight-fitting slacks, who elbowed their way slowly towards the center of the platform, politely apologizing as they squeezed through the packed throng. The third youth was taller, with slanted eyes and a sardonic smile that twisted his lips. He was very pale and he darted nervous glances about him as he followed his two companions through the crowd.

It was Lynx. Now Charles knew why he had been summoned.

He had heard arguments between Kléber, Vidal, and Lynx, bitter quarrels that had gone on for hours. The Communists' primary concern was to keep as many German troops as possible in France and away from the Russian front. They were pleading for sabotage in the factories making war goods, for propaganda among the Fritzes to sow dissension, and finally for armed attack on German officers. This was Lynx's argument: Kill the Nazis and they won't dare withdraw any troops from France.

Patiently, Vidal—with Kléber a grumbling second—had pointed out the weakness of the

Resistance: few men and fewer arms. To attack the Germans openly was suicide. For every officer shot down, they would execute a hundred, if need be a thousand, innocent men and women. Hostages and reprisals—the arithmetic would be murderous.

"It is not you or I who will bear the brunt of this," Vidal had said soberly. "It will always be possible to plan an ambush, shoot down the unsuspecting victim, and get away cleanly. But to pay for this 'patriotic' deed, the Germans will empty the jails and prisons of curfew violators, black-market dealers, and people who tried to cross the demarcation line to see a relative or parent. And, if needed, there are always helpless Jews to add to the lists destined for the firing squads, or . . ." Vidal had paused and stared cruelly at Lynx. "Or Communists now in French jails. Is that what you want?"

Lynx had flinched under the terrible stare and mumbled something about reprisals bringing more people into the underground struggle, about "the blood of martyrs."

Kléber had snorted contemptuously. "Your kind makes damned certain that their own blood never mixes with that of martyrs." The argument had ended with Lynx stalking out of the printing shop, thwarted and furious.

And to avenge that taunt, Lynx needed a witness to what was about to happen. Charles knew he had been selected because he would be helpless to stop it.

Lynx paused behind a stocky German sergeant who was explaining the Paris subway system to a new recruit. For a long moment, as Charles watched with mounting horror, he stared at the back of the German's head as if trying to read something on the close-cropped skull. Finally, he licked his lips and moved slightly back into the mob. There was no mistaking the look of fanatical hatred on his face.

The automatic barrier door started to hiss and swing shut. At the last minute, a German naval officer in dress whites slipped past the closing door, smiling triumphantly. As he worked his way to the center of the platform where the first-class car would halt, he passed directly in front of Lynx. *Like Bonsergent,* Charles thought in despair, *fate has brought him here, to this very spot, and stood him in front of his murderer.* There was nothing Charles could do but stand and watch a play the ending of which he already knew.

There was a rumbling sound down the tunnel as the train approached. Soon its lights could be seen; then, with a squeal, it came around the turn, rolled along the platform, and stopped with a jolt. The doors of the white first-class car opened quickly and the naval officer moved forward to enter.

What happened next took place so quickly that all the actions seemed to blend together. To a horrified Charles, it seemed to be a series of jerky frames from an old movie with everything slowed down and unsynchronized. First, the German moved forward so desperately slowly, as if he could never reach the door. As he lifted his foot to step into the train, Lynx took his hand very,

71

very slowly from the pocket of his windbreaker. There was something black and shiny in it that he pressed against the back of the white uniform. The explosions were muffled, as if the sound track had been badly scratched at that point. The young officer arched his back violently (it was the only fast action in this strange film), twisted against the door, and slipped, face down, half in and half out of the train. By the time his cap had rolled to the back of the car, Lynx was gone.

Suddenly the film speeded up. A woman, her face distorted with fear, screamed again and again while the German sergeant ran from the train, clutching at his gun holster. The crowd moved back from the motionless form, and Charles could see the two red stains on the back of the white jacket. He slipped along the wall of the platform, careful not to attract attention. Cursing and striking out when they ran into people, two soldiers pushed their way towards the exit, yelling for the military police. Other soldiers clustered around the red-faced sergeant, who was kneeling by the body. Charles wormed his way through the crowd and out the exit. He forced himself to walk slowly out of the subway, giving way to the German policemen who came racing down the steps.

He walked down the Boulevard Barbès, then turned into a side street and found a café that looked empty. Pale and exhausted, he tried to keep the panic out of his voice as he ordered a glass of wine. He drained the glass and shuddered as the cold liquid flowed down his throat. *My God,* he thought, *there is no warmth left in*

*wine now. Macbeth has murdered sleep . . .
no, Lynx has murdered a German officer.* Charles
could not shake the sight of those two ugly red
roses from his mind.

"He didn't even change expression," Charles
told Vidal and Kléber. "Just that same tight,
twisted smile he always has. Anyone watching
would have thought that he was pushing the German ahead of him into the train. Then he fired. . . ."

Vidal shook his head gravely and the old man
cursed, showing a command of profanity that
made Seagull blush. She walked away from the
angry diatribe and sat at a table in the corner.
Charles gripped his knees tighter and tried to
control the tremor in his voice. "I don't think anyone saw him. His two lookouts were ready to
cover his escape, but there was no need for them.
Lynx was out of the station before the Fritz hit
the ground. And he wanted me there as a witness."

"Damn right!" Kléber spat disgustedly. "One,
he wanted a witness so that we would know who
did this glorious deed, and, two, he was jealous of
you. He had to show you in particular what a
hero he was." The old man shot a significant
glance at Seagull.

Vidal took a piece of paper out of his pocket
and handed it to Charles. "I found that on my
desk when I arrived just before seven this morning. More than an hour before the shooting."

It was typed on the same cheap lined paper.
The message was short: "We got even for Porcupine!"

"So it was revenge?" Charles could not keep the doubt from his voice.

Vidal shook his head vigorously. "No, not revenge. Orders from the Central Committee, probably." He slumped into a chair and hid his head in his hands under Kléber's pitying gaze. "It won't end here, either. There will be another and another, and the Germans will slaughter thousands in their rage. Horrible, horrible."

They sat there in stunned silence, listening to the crackle of the wood fire. Finally the old man whispered something in Vidal's ear and the two men left the room. *There are plans to be made, instructions to be given,* Charles thought. *This is a new war now, an armed struggle forced on us by this stupid deed. And the Germans have all the guns.*

He went over to the table where Seagull was industriously writing. She looked up as he approached and gave him a wan smile.

"The truly terrible thing," Charles said, "is that they picked their victim by pure chance. He wasn't a Gestapo agent or a collaborator or someone who was an immediate threat to them. For all they knew—or cared—he could have been a teacher inducted against his will, possibly even anti-Nazi. But because wore a German uniform, they condemned him to death. All right, I can accept that. He was an enemy soldier, and if he didn't want to die, he should have stayed at home. But now they will shoot innocent people. And Lynx and his friends will shoot another Fritz . . ." His voice died away.

The girl brushed a stray lock of hair from her

face and pursed her lips thoughtfully. "It had to come sooner or later. It is naïve to think that we will get rid of the Nazis without killing on both sides. It is a shock only because it came sooner than we expected. Lynx and his friends are right. It is our fault that we were not prepared. In spite of what happened to Porcupine, we have been playing at war like children. Now we will have to fight it like real soldiers . . . if necessary to the death."

She picked up her papers and left the room without another word. Behind her, Charles stared flabbergasted at her empty chair. That she should defend Lynx! That was what hurt, not that she should accuse him of being naïve. For now he knew one truth about himself: he was jealous.

The next day, the Germans posted a large reward "for information leading to the arrest of the cowardly assassin of the German naval officer in the Barbès subway station." The population was warned that any further attacks on German soldiers would lead to the most severe measures being taken, including the execution of hostages now in German hands. The frightened Parisians discussed this new turn of events. There were rumors that the Germans were arresting people at random on the streets to be certain that hostages would be ready if the need arose. As far as Charles could determine from his contacts in different parts of the city, these rumors were groundless. The Nazis had no need for new arrests; the jails were already packed swollen with minor offenders who had fallen foul of the numerous petty regulations.

"Lynx is gone," Charles reported to a worried Vidal three days later. "Either he is in hiding or he has left the city. In any case, we can't find a trace of him anywhere, and none of his old friends have seen him since the shooting—or so they say."

"So now all we can do is wait and see where he surfaces next," the scar-faced man said. Then he reprimanded Charles for making an unauthorized search.

The days that followed were nerve-wracking. Charles could feel the tension in the city; people talked in low voices in the bars and restaurants, and jumped whenever a truck backfired. The Germans were the most nervous, since they were the immediate targets of the hidden gunmen. They were always armed now, and never ventured out after dark except in groups of two or three or more. The patrols had been strengthened and were so jittery that stray cats and dogs became casualties of indiscriminate gunfire in the darkness.

Everyone was waiting for the inevitable second attack.

It came two weeks later, but not in Paris. In the seaport town of Nantes on the Atlantic coast, the German commander and his adjutant had just left their office late at night and were about to enter their car when two men slipped out of the shadows behind them. In the furious burst of fire, the elderly colonel fell, mortally wounded. His aide was badly hit but managed to return the fire. The assailants disappeared, one of them limping.

This time the Germans did not bother with warnings, threats, or promises of rewards. The execution posters were on the walls of Paris the next day.

"Here, take it!" Charles shouted. He thrust a copy of the death notice at a startled Seagull. Furious, he had torn it from the wall where it had been freshly pasted and carried it to the printing shop. "Here is what the brave Lynx has accomplished. Go on, look at it!"

Silently, the girl picked up the long sheet and read the list.

"Are you still proud of him? One hundred men! One hundred Frenchmen, innocent of any crime! They pulled them out of the prisons and shoved them in front of firing squads at dawn this morning. One hundred—for one lousy German! Did they teach you arithmetic in your school? How many French men and women will have to die if we shoot down all the Germans in France?"

Pale and shaken, the girl did not answer. Charles' fury mounted. He felt a terrible need to humiliate her, to grind her face in this awful atrocity, as if she were to blame for it. "Take a look at these last three names! The Fritzes want us to know who they shot: Guy Môquet, seventeen years old; Anton Lebussier, seventeen years old; Jean Delombe, sixteen years old . . ."

The girl began to sob, her thin body shaking. For a moment, Charles looked down at her with pity. Gently, he took the poster out of her hand, but when he spoke, his voice was still harsh and unforgiving.

"You're right about one thing, though. It had to come to this sooner or later. But Lynx and his friends might have waited until we were ready to fight back."

5

Charles spotted the Englishman immediately in the crowd of travelers coming off the train from Marseilles. He looked exactly as Vidal had described him: "Tall, well-built, about forty. He'll be wearing a gray raincoat and a soft hat and will be carrying a briefcase with a handle wrapped in red paper." Well, there he was—fifteen minutes late—standing at the exit gate like a lost soul. Hadn't anyone told him that railroad stations were filled with Gestapo agents, Vichy policemen, and plain stool pigeons—all waiting to pounce on anyone who looked the least bit suspicious?

The Englishman looked startled as Charles approached, his hand extended in greeting. Clearly, the man from London had not expected his contact to be so young.

Charles spoke first. "Welcome to Paris, M. Gilbert. I trust your aunt is better?"

Shifting his briefcase, the agent grasped Charles' hand in a surprisingly strong grip. He gave the second part of the recognition message in a well-modulated, cultured voice. "She is very well now, thank you. You were very kind to meet me at such an early hour." *His French is not bad,*

Charles thought, *just the faintest touch of an accent that is hard to identify. He could pass for a professor from the Midi, Lyons, or Limoges, maybe.*

They chatted as they walked to the newspaper stand in the center of the waiting room. They discussed the weather (rainy), the food situation (worsening every week), and the activities of several imaginary friends. The Englishman was clearly delighted to be in Paris—"The first time in fifteen years," he said—and seemed to be oblivious to the danger that surrounded them. Charles smiled indulgently while he went on and on about his feelings for the city, but as the minutes passed and the second agent did not appear, Charles' nervousness increased. They could not stand around much longer pretending to look at newspapers and magazines.

"Your friend?" Charles' question was accusing.

The Englishman glanced casually at the crowd still coming through the gate from the train and shrugged his shoulders. His lack of concern irritated Charles. *Where the hell does he think he is?* Charles thought. *This isn't London. He's not in Waterloo Station with nothing to worry about but German bombers overhead. There will be no siren to warn him of danger.*

"We thought it best not to travel in the same carriage," the British agent said, "just in case of a check. Pascal must have gone a long way back to find a seat. . . . Ah, here he is."

The man who came through the exit gate carrying an old suitcase was perspiring freely. Medium height, round face with a thick brush mustache;

he grunted at each step as he made his way past the newspaper stand without stopping or glancing in their direction. *At least this one is smart enough to be afraid,* Charles thought, *but does he have to show it? He looks like a black-market butcher smuggling beef in that suitcase.*

Charles nodded to the Englishman and they fell into step behind the sweating Pascal. As they mingled with the noisy crowd moving towards the main entrance of the Gare d'Austerlitz, Gilbert resumed his paean of praise for the glories of Paris; Charles looked around carefully for the enemy.

Charles was only half listening to the chatter when he sensed a slowing in the forward motion of the crowd ahead. Instantly he gripped the Englishman by the arm and pushed him forward until they were directly behind the second man. "Put down the suitcase and pretend you're fixing the lock," he hissed into Pascal's ear. With a startled glance over his shoulder, the round-faced agent obeyed.

As the crowd shuffled past them, Charles looked quickly at the side exits, but he already knew what he would see. The French police were blocking the doors and allowing no one to leave. There were protests from the travelers, but the police were inflexible. There would be no exit from the station except through the main entrance. The baggage-check counter had been closed.

"What is it?" the Englishman asked mildly.

Charles looked around him, his mind racing furiously. Unless he could find some way of getting them through the only exit allowed, they were done for.

"It's a *rafle*—a roundup," he said tersely. "They've got the station sealed off and the main entrance blocked. They're examining all identity cards and searching all packages and suitcases."

"My God," the sweaty little man moaned. "If they open this suitcase, we're lost."

"Be quiet," the Englishman said in the same even tone. "Will it be the French police?"

Charles nodded. "But there will be Gestapo men nearby in case they come up with anything that interests the Fritzes . . . like arms, or what you have in there." He tilted his chin towards the suitcase. "And they've closed the checkroom, so we can't leave it and pick it up later. It's either abandon the suitcase or try to get it past a search." Even as he was talking, Charles had settled on a plan—a desperate plan, but the only one he could think of that had the slightest chance.

He leaned over as if to help with the suitcase and whispered to Pascal, "Leave it. Go through the barrier and, in the name of God, stop sweating! Your papers are in order, and even if they search you there is nothing compromising on you, is there?" His eyes glazed with terror, the little man shook his head and, when Charles nodded towards the entrance, rose quickly to his feet and almost ran forward.

The Englishman watched his companion disappear into the crowd, then turned with a sigh towards Charles. "And what do I do, old man?"

"Act indignant at the outrage. How dare they

treat you like a common criminal? You have friends, powerful friends, in Paris, and you will report this to them. Demand to see the police card of the man searching you. Get his name and number. Once you've done that, get out fast. You must be out of sight before they begin on me. You and Pascal wait for me at the subway entrance. If I'm not there in ten minutes, go around the corner to the Café Denis, rue Sauvage, and ask for Labru. Understood?"

The Englishman nodded vaguely, but the puzzled smile persisted on his lips. Clearly, the logic of Charles' plan had escaped him. "And the suitcase?"

"I'll take it through," Charles said calmly. "But remember, no matter what, *you must see that police card,* and when you do, repeat the name and number aloud."

"I think I understand," Gilbert said. "Good luck." He turned and headed for the main entrance. Charles picked up the heavy suitcase and followed at a leisurely pace. He wanted at least three or four people ahead of him before the Englishman reached the barrier.

As they approached the main entrance, Charles took in the scene at a glance. The passengers had been formed into three lines and were being passed, one by one, through the openings in the police cordon. There was a plainclothes detective at each position examining parcels, luggage, and briefcases, and making a body search of the men. The women were being sent to a side room where a matron was waiting. To make certain that no one could rush through the blockade, a solid phalanx of policemen stood thirty feet behind the barrier, ready to grab a desperate runner. Three grim-faced men in the long black leather coats that the Gestapo favored stood among them, watching everything, missing nothing.

In the left-hand line, the Englishman was going into his performance. From his position four places back, Charles could hear every word, and he had to grin at the genuine outrage the soft-spoken agent managed to get into his voice. "This is insupportable. . . . You shall hear from the minister about this, my good man. . . . Do I look like a criminal? . . . I have friends, powerful friends. . . . The prefect of police himself will be told. . . . I demand to see your identification card!" The bored detective delved into the briefcase, ran his hands over the Englishman's body, then with a sneer flashed his police card. "Ah, very good. You have not heard the end of this, Gaston Pelletier, Number 1792," the agent proclaimed. He grabbed his briefcase from the examination table, shook his finger in the detective's face, and strode quickly through the police lines and out of the station.

What a ham he is, Charles thought. Still, it had been a very convincing performance.

It took only a few minutes for the people ahead of him to go through. Charles handed the detective his identity card and waited.

"Where are you coming from?" The question was being asked for the fiftieth time in the same bored tone.

"Montargis," Charles answered politely. "I was visiting a school chum of mine."

"What's in the suitcase?"

Charles lifted the heavy valise onto the table and opened it, making certain that the lifted top hid its contents from the Gestapo watchers and that his own body shielded it from the travelers patiently standing behind him. As the detective leaned forward to search, Charles bent over politely to help.

A pile of clean shirts, some socks and neckties . . . the detective pushed them aside and froze. Underneath was a large gray metal box covered with dials, coils, switches, and a loop of copper wire. A radio transmitter!

"Listen carefully," Charles whispered coldly, "and you may come out of this alive." As he bent over the suitcase, his lips were only inches from the detective's ear. "My friend has your name and number, remember? If anything happens to me or this suitcase, you're a dead man. The Resistance knows how to deal with French cops who are too zealous in helping the Germans."

With shaking hands, the detective slammed shut the lid of the suitcase and glanced nervously about to see if anyone had noticed. No one had. Charles' cold tone had clearly convinced him that he was in terrible danger. If they could shoot down German officers regardless of the cost . . . With a visible effort he handed back the identity card and jerked his thumb towards the exit.

Charles was in no hurry. He locked the suitcase carefully, pocketed his card, and shook hands with the flabbergasted policeman. Then he walked nonchalantly through the police lines, smiling politely at one of the Gestapo agents as he squeezed past him and out of the station.

The "safe house" was above a garage high up in Montmartre. The owner was a friend, a sympathizer, who had offered the location because radio transmissions needed high ground. When Charles arrived with Gilbert and Pascal, a tall, burly worker opened the door for them without a word and disappeared. It was a small three-room apartment furnished with a few worn, stained pieces of furniture, a threadbare carpet, and some hideous lithographs that made the Englishman wince.

The British agent had not stopped talking since they had left the subway and begun the long climb up the hill. In spite of Charles' tactful attempts to cut him off, the whole story of his life and career as a spy had been told in great detail.

His real name was Edward Dundridge; he was forty-four years old and a bank manager in Glasgow. As a young man he had been a clerk in his bank's office in Paris and, being of a serious turn of mind, had studied the language assiduously to earn promotion. "When the war broke out, I was seconded to the Paymaster Corps, but I couldn't bear sitting behind a desk while the other chaps were fighting. I was too old for the R.A.F., so when this officer came around and told me my knowledge of France could be of great help to the war effort, well, naturally. . ." His voice died away in an embarrassed silence as he tried to make light of his desire for action.

They had sent him to a secret school in Wales to learn his new trade: ciphers, collecting military information, use of explosives for sabotage: "I can blow up a building with nothing more than the stuff I carry in my pockets."

Although he disapproved of the Englishman's lack of discretion, Charles was fascinated by this glimpse of what went on across the Channel. After fifteen months in the Resistance, he had a professional interest in clandestine work. He asked questions about the organization of the British intelligence networks in France, how liaison was kept between them, and how they were supplied with arms, money, and propaganda materials. For the first time he became aware of the other *réseaux*—the little groups, scattered across both the occupied and unoccupied zones, that had formed spontaneously in response to the defeat and were now being coordinated and supplied by London. *So we are not alone,* he thought with pride.

Pascal had set up his radio in the little back bedroom and was making his first tentative contacts with London when Vidal and Kléber arrived just before four o'clock. The introductions were rather formal, and Vidal cut short the Englishman's enthusiastic description of how Charles had gotten the radio set out of the railroad station. "Never mind all that. It's here, so let's use it."

Gathered around the table in the bedroom, they watched tensely as Pascal fiddled with the dials, making his last adjustments. *He's stopped sweating now,* Charles noted, *but there is a tic in his right eye and his left hand is trembling. How can he work that key in this state?*

According to the Englishman, Pascal was a

Canadian and half French. He had been a sergeant in the Royal Signal Corps and had been through the hell of Dunkirk before volunteering for intelligence work. He and Pascal had met for the first time at the school in Wales, had been briefed together for this mission, and then had parachuted into the unoccupied zone at the first moon. The reception committee had had a truck waiting to take them to the railroad station in Marseilles. Except for some nervousness—"After all, this is the first time for both of us"—when their papers had been examined at the demarcation line, Pascal had been fine.

He doesn't look fine, Charles thought, *he looks damned scared.* He caught Kléber's eye and indicated the radio operator hunched feverishly over his set. The old man shrugged. Charles knew Kléber did not think too highly of the British and their sporting attitude towards war.

"Dah-dah-dit-dah." The faint staccato rhythm filled the silent room. Pascal adjusted the earphones to pick up the weak transmission, pounded out his acknowledgment, and began to scribble on the pad in front of him. The message was short and quickly decoded: "M-A-R-S-T-O-G-I-L-B-E-R-T-R-E-P-O-R-T."

The Englishman had his answer ready and coded. "Arrived safely. Missed rendezvous with Max. Train late. Request instructions. Gilbert."

There was a long silence as Mars digested this information. Vidal went to the window and peered nervously around the edge of the shade. *He's worried about the Fritzes picking up the signal,* Charles thought. Kléber had taught them that even if a radio is not transmitting, the carrier wave can be spotted by two or more German radio locators in vans. *It will only take them fifteen minutes to get a fix on this location. Why doesn't London answer? Don't they realize the danger?*

The radio sputtered to life again. Pascal scribbled the message, acknowledged receipt quickly, and switched off the set. The second message was longer: "Imperative Max be contacted second rendezvous and transfer made. Give this to Vidal. Your task German air strength Paris region. Next transmission 0710 hours tomorrow. Padre sends his greetings. End. Mars."

The Englishman smiled at the last sentence. "Good old Padre. He was my briefing officer. Worried too much about me, I guess."

"If he keeps us on the air with personal messages," Vidal said coldly, "he won't have to worry much longer. The Germans will see to that. I suppose next we can expect the latest cricket scores." The Englishman's smile died and he looked chagrined at the reprimand. "What's this about a second rendezvous with Max that I'm to take care of?" Vidal did not have to ask who Max was. Even the Germans knew the code name of the legendary leader of the Resistance in the unoccupied zone.

"I was to meet Max in Lyons the day after I arrived. I had an envelope with orders for him. Unfortunately, the train was over an hour late getting there and I knew he wouldn't wait, so I continued on to Paris. The second rendezvous is planned for Vichy on the twelfth—that's in three days."

Vidal nodded. "Where's the envelope?"

"In the suitcase." The Englishman slit the fabric in the lid of the suitcase and handed a thin envelope to Vidal, who shoved it into the inside pocket of his jacket without looking at it.

"We'll see that it is delivered," said Vidal. "When we find a suitable courier, you'll give him the time and place of the rendezvous, the recognition phrases, and a description of Max. Until then, don't wander about Paris. We don't want you picked up in a *rafle*." The scar-faced man's grin was mirthless. "Try to control your enthusiasm for our fair city. Later on, we'll make arrangements to give you a guided tour of the principal places of interest, like German airfields and Luftwaffe depots. Meanwhile, there will be two of our men on guard at all times—one in the garage and one on the corner. Keep the shades drawn and your voices low, and in the name of heaven, keep those radio messages short. If London gets too wordy, cut them off. Ten minutes is the limit, do you hear? Ten minutes, or you'll get an unpleasant guided tour of Gestapo headquarters—and not by us!"

The radio operator started to sweat again and he had trouble folding the copper wire antenna into the suitcase. Chastened, Gilbert promised to obey the rules. He looked so downcast that Charles felt sorry for him, but he knew that Vidal was only trying to keep the two agents alive. For a split second, he had a glimpse of Dundridge naked, strapped to a chair in that awful cellar with bloody stripes covering his body. Oh, he would be brave enough; British courage was proverbial. No doubt he would die with that empty smile on his lips. But Pascal would talk before the first blow was struck. Charles was convinced of it.

Later that afternoon, back at the printing shop, Kléber told Charles that he was to go to Vichy and keep the rendezvous with Max. Since a young couple would be less suspicious and because Seagull knew the crossing points on the demarcation line, she would accompany him. It was clear from his furious expression that the latter decision had been made over the old man's violent objections.

"Let's go over the whole thing just one more time," Seagull pleaded.

Charles threw up his arms in mock despair. Stretched out on the floor of his apartment, the map between them, they had rehearsed the trip, the crossing of the demarcation line, and the rendezvous with Max. But the girl's seriousness pleased him; he had never known anyone besides himself who was so thorough in detail. Being alone with her, caught up in the intimacy of planning their trip together, made his heart beat faster.

"We leave here at five in the morning, as soon as the curfew ends," he began. "The subway will take us to Ivry, where we hop a bus for Fontainebleau. There we get on the train for the south at 1010, arriving in Moulins—if there are no delays—at 1805." As he spoke, Charles again traced their route on the large-scale map. Seagull listened carefully. "We'll travel in the same compartment but as strangers to each other. In fact,

I'll probably try to flirt with you, and you can re-buff me haughtily."

"There's no point to that," she objected. "A boy and a girl on a camping trip together is nothing unusual. Besides, someone may see us on the bus and then wonder at this charade."

Charles sighed wearily. His little joke had gone completely over her head. "All right, we travel to-gether all the way. Now, Moulins is right on the demarcation line, so security will be very strict, but there should be no check except for those who are continuing on. If we're asked, we are camping along the river west of the town—which is true. You have selected the crossing point, but we can't go through until after dark, which means after 2300."

"How do we know when it is safe to cross?" the girl asked.

She's testing me, Charles thought. *She knows the answer as well as I do; after all, she is the ex-pert on sneaking across the line, and she knows this area like the back of her hand.*

"The Fritzes patrol the area in sections with a different schedule every day. We have to time them for at least five or six passes at the place where we want to cross. Also, we'll be able to see the French guards on the other side. Once we have their routine for that night, we'll have about six minutes to get across and under cover. That means we have to run about a kilometer in six minutes—in the dark, carrying knapsacks."

"Travel light, Falcon," the girl said with a taunting smile. "I promise you that it will seem like ten kilometers before you're finished."

Charles ignored the hint that he was not in condition and continued. "On the other side we wait in the woods until first light, then walk into Souvigny. There is a bus leaving at 0625 that will get us into Vichy around 1400. Since our appointment is not until 1715, we'll have to kill some time in town, ideally without attracting attention. I see no problem there. Vichy, after all, is the seat of our so-called government, if you can call that pack of collaborators a government. The place is crawling with officials, job-seekers, generals, ambassadors, profiteers, and tourists. No one will notice two or more campers passing through unless we call attention to ourselves."

Charles tossed his pencil on the map and rolled over on his back. "After we make the transfer, we come back by train all the way. We should be back in Paris in three days."

"Where is the envelope?"

"I folded it into a glassine packet and buried it in the bottom of a can of foot powder in my knapsack. Unless they cut open the can, they'll never find it."

He stared up at the ceiling and tried to keep his voice nonchalant. "By the way, what is your real name?"

Even without turning his head, he felt the girl stiffen. There was an awkward silence as she considered the question.

"After all," he continued, "it would seem very strange if some *flic* asked me that same question and I didn't know the answer. He'll know it from your identity card."

The explanation was reasonable enough, but he

sensed the struggle that was going on inside her. A code name like "Seagull" was anonymous and safe. Besides, she had been trained never to reveal her true identity to her comrades. If one of them was arrested and talked under torture, only the name "Seagull" would be revealed.

"My name is Charles Marceau," he said encouragingly. "Just in case they ask."

"Marie-Josette Loubet," she said reluctantly.

He rolled over, raised himself on his elbows, and stared at her admiringly. "Loubet, is it? Any relation to the late president of the Republic?"

"I can assure you that no relative of mine ever lived in the Élysées Palace," she said tartly. "My father was a mailman in the Compiègne district of Paris."

"Was?"

"He was killed on the first day of the fighting."

Charles felt his face flush with embarrassment. He tried to reach out and touch her arm to show his sympathy, but she moved away slightly. She stared for a moment into the fireplace, then went on.

"And—in case they should ask—I work as a salesgirl at the Grand Louvre, selling cheap jewelry mostly. I live at 27 rue Florian near the Père Lachaise cemetery. I have a roommate named Yvonne who works with me during the day at the Grand Louvre and spends her nights in the bars in Pigalle. She's lonely; her fiancé has been in a prisoner-of-war camp for almost eighteen months now. For a few drinks, she—"

"Please, Marie-Josette," Charles pleaded. "No more. I'm sorry."

She stood up and brushed off her skirt and blouse. "We have to be up early, so I'm going to bed. Good night, Charles Marceau." She went into his parents' bedroom and closed the door.

Confused, Charles stared into the fire. The question had been legitimate, but it should have been put more delicately. He had failed to understand that private world of sadness she carried within her. Seagull and Falcon had been comrades in the underground struggle, but Marie-Josette Loubet and Charles Marceau—what would they be? He slammed his fist down, ripping the corner of the map.

Ten minutes later, he tapped timidly on her door.

"Come in." Her tone was neutral, almost indifferent.

When he entered, she looked up questioningly from her book. *She seems so small in that big bed,* he thought. He cleared his throat several times, then said hoarsely, "I—uh—forgot to tell you. In case they come tonight . . ." He knew that he was babbling and the thought made him even tenser. "You know, the Gestapo . . ." The girl nodded. "Well, the best way out is—uh—through that window and up the fire escape to the—uh—roof."

Charles stopped and made a feeble gesture towards the window. He could see the outline of her body under the sheet. It bothered him; he felt as if he had no right to see it.

"Mademoiselle, I am truly sorry. I did not mean to intrude. Please forgive me if you can."

He turned and started to close the door.

"Charles."

This time her voice was soft and friendly again. He halted in the doorway, but did not dare look at her.

"My friends call me Majo."

He closed the door quickly.

6

As soon as the bus left the village of Souvigny and started its climb up the poplar-lined road to Vichy, Charles fell asleep. His head flopped from side to side as the *gazogène* bucked and jolted along. He looked so uncomfortable that Seagull took pity on him, drew him closer, and let him sleep on her shoulder.

So far, the trip had been without incident, and they were even an hour ahead of schedule. The crossing of the demarcation line had been surprisingly simple; the German patrol and the French frontier guards had stuck to their schedule and the two young people had slipped out of their hiding place, crossed the stream and the wheat field, and taken shelter in the woods in the unoccupied zone with minutes to spare. As they had walked into Souvigny, a gendarme on a bicycle had sped past them with only a brief suspicious glance. When they had smiled and waved to him, he had shrugged his shoulders and continued on his way. Two more crazy kids sleeping in the fields—there was nothing strange in that these days.

Every twenty kilometers, the puffing *gazogène*

stopped while the driver shoveled charcoal into the huge cast-iron boiler on the roof, then went snorting on. At each of the villages on the way, the bus halted to unload passengers and cargo. A few people got on, mostly farmers on their way to the regular Wednesday market in town. Only once, on the outskirts of Vichy itself, were their papers checked. The gendarme barely glanced at the proffered I.D. cards, made a perfunctory search of the baskets and parcels, and, yielding to the girl's smile, did not wake Charles. In what was laughingly called the "free" zone, Seagull knew, a sense of urgency was lacking. In Paris, they would all have been lined up on the road and thoroughly searched.

It was a little after three o'clock when the bus shuddered to a halt in the town square. A cloud of steam poured from under the hood and the engine seemed to give up the ghost.

"Vichy!" the driver bawled. "Seat of the government, home of the French State and Marshal Pétain. Baths, medicinal waters, and sure cures for sluggish livers!" Charles woke with a start and peered sleepily about. The girl handed him his knapsack and they descended into the crowded marketplace. "Stay with the crowd," she whispered, "just in case the police are watching."

The stalls past which they strolled were filled with a profusion of foods that had long since disappeared from the grocery stores in Paris. Charles stared in amazement at the piles of pears, apples, cherries, and oranges; the large hams, chickens, and rabbits; the combs of golden honey; the mushrooms, even truffles; all the farms in France seemed to have poured their abundance onto the counters. "In Paris we get two pounds of potatoes," Charles said bitterly, "a few rutabagas, four pounds of bread, and eight ounces of meat—when it is available—a week! But here . . ." He pointed to a mountain of cabbages and lettuce topped with tomatoes and onions.

Seagull licked her lips at the sight of some luscious melons. "In Paris and the rest of the occupied zone," she explained, "the Germans take all the food; first they feed their soldiers and then they ship the rest to Germany. Down here in the unoccupied zone, there is plenty of food, but the farmers don't want to pay the Vichy taxes or obey the numerous regulations, so they bring their produce into town and trade it for cigarettes, pipe tobacco, razor blades, a pair of shoes or a dress, anything that can't be found in the shops. And what you see is only part of what our patriotic peasants are hoarding. When the black-market profiteer comes to the back door with his truck, he gets not hams but whole pigs, dozens of plucked chickens, butter by the churnful, and the best of the local wines by the case. For this he pays through the nose, big fat banknotes, but the farmers are happy because the Vichy tax inspectors don't know about it, and the profiteer is happy because he can sell it in the occupied zone for three times what he paid for it. Meanwhile, the little people starve, sucked dry by the Boches up north and their own countrymen down here."

"Well, if anyone here deserves to eat well, it's you and me," Charles said belligerently. He dug his extra shirt out of his knapsack and walked over to a fruit stand run by a dumpy woman with a large hairy mole on her nose. The shirt was a fine hand-embroidered one that his mother had given him, and by dint of hard bargaining it brought four oranges, six apples, and a small bag of cherries. "And it's not even my son's size," the old woman grumbled as she stuffed the shirt into her basket.

"Don't forget to declare its fair value to the tax man," Charles shot over his shoulder as he and Majo walked away. She jerked his arm. He was making himself conspicuous both by his loud bargaining and by the taunt.

They walked out of the square eating the cherries and enjoying themselves immensely. Surrounded though they were by the symbols of a France degraded by defeat, a France that tried to curry favor with the conqueror by collaboration, the two young people refused to be downhearted. The day was bright and sunny, with a warm breeze. Everywhere there were brilliant reds and yellows—the fruits in the stalls, the colorful country clothing, even the buildings. In the distance above the town, Charles and Majo could see the blue-gray of the mountains, for Vichy is on a high plateau where the Grand Massif range starts its rise. Wisps of clouds floated by. It was a glorious October day and they had tacitly agreed not to think of Max or the underground struggle for two more hours.

A hotel stood catty-corner from the exit to the square, and a large crowd gathered in front of it were watching the door. They were talking in low, respectful tones as if they were standing before a church on a holy day. "What's that all about?" Charles asked, spitting out a pit.

"That's the Hôtel du Parc," Majo replied. "Pétain's headquarters. They're waiting for a glimpse of the Marshal. The chief of state, the Victor of Verdun."

"Verdun he did defend in the First World War—although my father insisted that he was ready to retreat when the Germans suddenly quit attacking—but chief of what state? Vichy exists because it serves the Fritzes' purpose. They could wipe it out in an hour, and, one day, they will."

Majo looked around them to see if anyone had been close enough to hear. "That's enough of that, Charles. Let's walk down by the river." He grinned mischievously at her warning. He was feeling very happy. In spite of the stigma of Frenchmen who would not fight, the town was lovely, filled with little parks and baths in the Oriental style, complete with minarets and cupolas. The mountain air made him light-headed. It was a beautiful day to be walking with a girl. He remembered the formal dances at which he had been introduced to the daughters of his parents' friends: stiff rigid ceremonies, with white gloves, patent leather shoes, and corsages. . . . He had gone through the whole painful routine of trying to waltz around with an unsmiling doll who had never said a word. It couldn't have been much fun for the girls either, but did they have to shove handkerchiefs down the fronts of their dresses to make believe they had bosoms?

Holding hands, Charles and Majo strolled through the side streets, peering into the shop windows and admiring the stately homes of the families who had made Vichy water famous throughout the world. No one seeing two flushed young campers openly gawking at the sights would have guessed that they were playing the most dangerous game of all.

Ten minutes before the scheduled meeting with Max, they took up their position on a park bench opposite the Grand Casino. The gamblers were long gone, for the casino was now a government building, military or naval if one judged by the uniforms of the men entering and leaving. Charles peeled an orange with his scout knife and shared it with Majo, and then went to a nearby trash can as if to drop the orange peels into it. A quick glance told him that he was unobserved. He took the can of foot powder from his knapsack, ripped open the side with the saw-toothed blade of his knife, shoved the glassine packet into his jacket sleeve, and buried the torn can, peels, and apple cores under the refuse in the container. Now he was ready for Max.

When he returned to the bench, Majo was stroking her cheek with the index finger of her left hand. It was the danger signal! Alert, Charles looked about for the threat.

There were only three people in sight—two housewives with shopping bags on the opposite bench, resting their weary feet, and an elderly gentleman in an old-fashioned morning coat standing about thirty yards down the path. He was peering through pince-nez at the botanical sign on one of the trees. The officers in front of the casino were too far away to be a menace, and the housewives too deep in conversation to notice them, so it had to be the man.

"The old gentleman?" he asked quietly.

Majo nodded and smiled as if he had offered a compliment. "I'm almost certain that he was next to us in front of the Hôtel du Parc. He must be following us."

Even as Charles watched, the two housewives, still chattering, rose and walked out of the park. As they passed behind the man, he turned and bowed slightly to them. Then he returned to his study of the tree. *Who is he?* Charles wondered. One of the secret Vichy police known as the *Milice* who were the Resistance's most avid opponents in the unoccupied zone?

"Look at his right-hand pocket," Majo whispered. There it was—the ominous bulge that Kléber had warned them of when they had been fledglings in the underground. Should they stay? Should they leave and miss warning Max? Charles felt the cold in the pit of his stomach as he struggled to find an answer. At that moment, the man turned and walked toward them, his hand in the bulging pocket.

"Kiss me!" Majo hissed fiercely. Flabbergasted, Charles stared at her, his mouth open. Had she gone mad?

She grabbed the lapels of his jacket and pulled him closer, her face lifted. Astonishment gave way to pleasure as he met the moist warmth of her lips. He slipped his arms about her waist and felt her yield. But even as he played the young lover, fear gripped him. It was hard to be romantic when any moment he expected to hear those terrible words: "German police! You're under arrest!" Without knowing it, he tightened the embrace.

"Take it easy, Charles," Majo muttered softly. "I said kiss me, not rape me in public." Chastened, he released her and muttered an apology.

"Mademoiselle. Monsieur." The trembling voice was a further dashing of cold water on Charles' fevered brow. Reluctantly, he turned and stared up questioningly at the elderly gentleman standing, hat in hand, in front of them. *The old geezer is awfully polite for a policeman,* he thought, dazed.

Clearing his throat, the old man bowed and continued. "I have been watching you for some time now. These are sad days for our poor country, but seeing you young people together like this somehow makes me believe that France will rise again. Please accept this little gift with my thanks for keeping France French." With that, he fumbled in his bulging pocket and slowly brought out a small paper bag. Carefully, he poured the contents into Majo's cupped hands, bowed again, and walked away.

They stared after him until he was lost to sight around the bend. "What is it?" Charles asked.

The girl began to giggle, then laughed wildly. "Look, look! Would you believe it? Chestnuts, roasted chestnuts!"

For a moment they could only look at each other in astonishment. Then relief flooded them and they doubled up with laughter. Some policeman—just an old fellow with romantic notions of young lovers! Charles wiped the tears from his eyes and looked fondly at Majo. She was still giggling spasmodically as she arranged her hair and straightened her blouse. He reached over and replaced a stray lock, letting his fingers stroke her cheek and her chin.

"Falcon." The tenseness in her voice jerked him from his reverie. "Here he comes."

The man was standing hesitantly in front of the casino, looking about as if lost. Then he turned and walked up the path towards them. From his appearance—medium height, balding in front, dressed in an inexpensive gray suit with vest and shiny black shoes—he could have been a minor official in one of the many government offices. Charles noted the two recognition signs immediately: the white scarf and the newspaper in the left jacket pocket.

As Max walked past them, paying no attention to the two young people on the bench, Charles glanced casually at him. A sensitive face—he looked rather artistic—deep-set eyes, and a fine bone structure . . . not what he had expected in the redoubtable Max, the head of the Resistance in the unoccupied zone. He should have been a military type, erect, commanding, a former officer.

"Wait until he is around the bend," he said quietly to Majo. He took the chestnuts from her hands and threw them over his shoulder into the bushes.

When Max had turned the corner in the path, Charles and Majo rose slowly and, hand in hand, followed. There was no need to hurry. Although Max was expecting the Englishman, he would know that the missed rendezvous had changed things, but that the transfer would take place at the spot previously agreed upon. He would wait there for them.

When they turned the corner in the path, the man in the gray suit was out of sight. The path led them out of the park, across a wide street, and then to the walk along the Allier River. The beaches were deserted—it was too late in autumn for swimming—but several small sailboats racing swiftly before the breeze played on the waters. Turning right, they strolled along, admiring the sunlit scene and carefully noting the few pedestrians they passed. It was all very ordinary, almost banal, but they could not forget their training: "When danger seems farthest away, it is closest. When you are relaxed and unsuspicious, that's when they will take you."

Max was leaning against the railing overlooking the beaches, a short pipe clenched in his teeth. He did not turn when the young couple strolled up next to him. Charles stood on Max's left so that his elbow brushed the newspaper.

"Excuse me, monsieur, can you tell me the way to the yacht club?" Charles asked politely.

Max pointed down the walk with his pipe, indicating the direction in which they had been walking. If he had pointed back the way they had come, it would have been a warning, a sign of danger, and they would have left without making the transfer. "It's that circular white building down there, the one with the blue flag above it."

"Ah yes, but the flag looks green." Even as he spoke, Charles reached surreptitiously into his sleeve, pulled out the envelope in its glassine packet, and slipped it between the folds of the newspaper.

With a resigned sigh, Max knocked his pipe against the railing and stared off across the river. "It does seem green, but it is blue." His tone was aggrieved, as if he resented the intrusion into his thoughts. His long slender fingers were adjusting the white scarf absentmindedly.

It was done. The mission was over. Charles thanked the "stranger" politely, took Majo's hand, and continued their walk towards the yacht club.

Twenty minutes later, they were on the train to Moulins, and Paris.

"Why do you suppose he was wearing a scarf on such a warm day?" Charles asked. Except for an elderly woman belligerently knitting against the sway of the railway coach, the car was empty. The conductor was half asleep in the rear seat, too far away to hear, but Charles kept his voice low.

"I heard the Englishman talking to Vidal about him," Majo whispered. "It seems he was the mayor of a small town in the north. In 1940, when the Germans entered, they tried to make him sign a document stating that French troops were responsible for an atrocity the Nazis had committed . . . twelve civilians shot down in cold blood. Max refused and they beat him up terribly, and then threw him into jail, threatening to shoot him if he did not sign. In his weakened condition, confused, alone, he was afraid that he could not hold out if they started torturing him again, but he couldn't disgrace himself and the

French army by signing. He smashed the window through the bars, and with a piece of glass . . ." Majo's voice broke and she shuddered. "With a piece of glass, he cut his throat!"

Charles swallowed hard and gripped the girl's hand reassuringly. A man like Max would cut his own throat for honor's sake. There had been a rumor that Porcupine had not died in front of a firing squad but had thrown himself out of the fourth-story window of Gestapo headquarters to keep from talking.

"Now he wears the scarf to hide the scars. The Fritzes found him in time and patched him up. He escaped later, but they have his description, and the scars are a dead giveaway." Majo's voice trembled with indignation . . . and pride. *What a man!* Charles thought. He wondered if it was permitted for a good Catholic to commit suicide in this battle for France. Better not to dwell on it and hope it never would come to that.

The train jolted violently, then began to slow. The conductor awoke and, peering out the window, announced, "Moulins. Everyone out for the border check."

Picking up their knapsacks, they descended from the train into the crowded station. The routine, they knew, was to have their papers checked by the French border guards, then walk across the footbridge over the river that marked the demarcation line, show their papers to the Germans there, and get on the train to Paris. Since their papers were in order and the envelope was gone, they had nothing to fear from even the most careful search.

But something was terribly wrong.

Instead of an orderly line of passengers moving past the inspection point, a protesting mob was clustered indignantly around a sweating station-master. "Ladies, please . . . gentlemen, I beg you . . . this is no fault of ours. The Germans have closed the border for the night. . . . We had no notice. . . . I beg you, please be calm. . . . Undoubtedly tomorrow you can continue. . . ."

Without a word, Charles and Majo walked around the crowd and out of the station. Across the street, they sat on a bus bench and took stock of the situation.

"We can cross where we did before," Majo suggested.

Charles shook his head firmly. "If the Fritzes closed the border, there is trouble on the other side. Maybe someone took a shot at a German officer. In any case, you can be certain that they'll be patrolling like mad all night—and not according to any schedule. Why take the risk of being picked up trying to slip across, when we have nothing to fear? Better to wait until morning and see if the border is open."

"We can't go to a hotel. That means filling out police cards, and besides, young campers don't do that."

"I know. And we don't have enough money for a hotel. No, it looks like we sleep out under the stars tonight. Agreed?"

Majo nodded her head. On this side of the river, Moulins was quite small. A fifteen-minute walk would take them out of town and into the

fields. If they were fortunate, some friendly farmer would let them use his barn. If not, they
could curl up under a hedge. Luckily, it did not
look like rain.

They found a barn, and later that night they
made love. There was no lust in it—just something
like affection, comrades comforting each other.
When it was over, they lay quietly side by side.

Majo sighed sleepily and pulled the blankets up
under her chin. In the darkness, he could just see
the pale oval of her face, the half-closed eyes. Her
lips were still slightly parted and he felt the
warmth of her breath against his cheek.

"Well?" Charles asked, brushing her lips with
his finger.

The girl twisted away and asked querulously,
"Well, what?"

"Have you nothing to say?"

This time she sat up. "What is there to say? Do
you expect me to explain something?" she demanded sleepily.

Refusing to be put off by her tone, he said in a
teasing voice, "In a very similar situation, Emma
Bovary cried out, 'I have a lover! I have a lover!' "

"All right," Majo said sweetly, "I have a lover. I
have a lover. I have a lover. Now I have one more
than your Emma What's-her-name, whoever she
may be."

"Bovary—the heroine of Flaubert's novel!"
Charles cried. "Surely you have heard of—"

"Look, Charles, we didn't do much reading of
the classics in my neighborhood—mostly detective
stories and cheap novels. I'm not apologizing; I'm

explaining. I went to work when I was fourteen because we needed the money. No doubt there are a lot of beautiful things I've missed so far, including the novels of this Flaubert, and after the war I hope to find out about them—although I must say that this Emma What's-her-name sounds like a very unattractive, hysterical type to me."

Charles smiled happily. What would his school principal, that old fussbudget Chailland, have said about this character analysis of the unfortunate Emma?

"As for our making love," Majo continued, "these things happen. You are very attractive, Charles—no, don't preen yourself on my words— and I am happy that you find me so. Well, if not attractive, at least desirable. It means a great deal to a woman from the rue Florian. You're not the usual type of skirt-chaser we have to deal with down there. No, you are very sweet and educated and even a trifle *naïf* . . . and don't start pouting, either; that is not a bad thing in a boy your age. But we have more important matters to worry about than these chance encounters, like, will the border be open tomorrow, and what has happened in Paris while we were gone. Now go to sleep like a good boy. Good night, Falcon."

She kissed him lightly on the lips to take some of the sting from her words, turned over, and buried her head under the blankets. Charles brooded over "chance encounters" for a few minutes, then shrugged his shoulders, yawned, and fell asleep.

He dreamed of a young woman dressed in a riding habit, stretched out on a grassy pasture near a windmill. He could not see her face as she twisted sensuously from side to side, but she was crying out over and over again that she had a lover.

It troubled him that he was nowhere in the picture.

The next morning they rose early, rolled their blankets and strapped them to the knapsacks. The grizzled old farmer who had let them use the barn sold them some bread, cheese, and two glasses of milk. With a sly smile, he asked how they had slept, and was assured that they had slept very well; then they said goodbye and started on the road to Moulins, eating their breakfast.

When they arrived at the footbridge over the river, the border was open. The German sergeant spent more time admiring Majo's figure than he did examining their papers. Charles felt hot words rising to his lips, but the girl poked him in the ribs, smiled sweetly at the amorous Fritz, and was rewarded with a chuck under the chin.

The train for Paris left one hour later. They arrived at the Gare d'Austerlitz in the early evening, just before the street lights went on. Outside the station, Majo shook hands solemnly with a sober Charles and disappeared into the crowd around the subway entrance.

He was so intent on watching her that he did not realize that someone was speaking to him. Then he recognized the voice and froze in panic.

"My congratulations, Marceau. You didn't lie to us after all. Your housemaid is a real beauty." Leaning against a pillar, Louis Engel—Blondie—

grinned mirthlessly as he jerked his thumb towards the subway. Beside him, the sullen-looking Gestapo agent who had been guarding the cellar listened impatiently.

Sick to his stomach, Charles forced himself to smile.

7

Charles turned the corner from the railroad station into the rue Sauvage. He did not have to look back to see if Blondie was following; by now he had developed the sixth sense that tells the hunted when the hunter is close by. Fear was threatening to choke him, and he swallowed several times and breathed deeply as he hurried down the narrow streets to the Café Denis.

It was little more than a side-street bar: a long counter, a few tables with red checkered tablecloths, a mirror on the far wall. It was crowded with early drinkers; most of the men in this working-class district stopped in for a glass of wine and a chat with their *copains* before going home to supper. No one paid any attention when Charles entered and walked to a table in the rear, least of all the bartender busy rinsing glasses, but he noticed that the radio had been turned up when he had entered, so that the noise drowned out all conversation. *That must be their signal,* he thought. In the Café Denis, as in a thousand other *bistros* in Paris, a stranger spelled trouble, and until he was identified, it was best that conversations not be overheard.

They kept him waiting for five minutes. Then the bartender came to his table and stood silently looking down at him.

"A glass of red wine," Charles ordered. "Do you have any St. Poulenc '38?"

"Hell no," the burly man growled, "and we don't have any '39 or '40 either. What do you think this is, some fancy restaurant on the Champs-Élysées?"

Charles sighed wearily. "All right, the house wine then . . . and ask M. Labru to have a glass with me."

The bartender leaned over to inspect a stain on the tablecloth. "I'm Labru."

"Falcon," Charles said tensely. "Tell our mutual friend that the operation was successful, but Blondie was at the railroad station when we got back. He saw both of us. I'll wait at the apartment."

"The house wine. OK." On his way back to the bar, the burly man nodded and someone turned down the radio. The tension in the room disappeared. This time it had been a friend and not a Gestapo stool pigeon.

Charles sipped his wine and listened idly to the pro-German program from Radio Paris. Once again the Nazis were supposed to be at the gates of Moscow and the American fleet had been sunk—for the third time—in a great Japanese naval victory in the Pacific. It was all old hat and very boring. He forced himself to relax in the hot, smoke-filled room. No one had entered the café since he had arrived, but he did not have to look at the front window to know that he was being watched. Maybe Blondie was trying to make up his mind whether it was worth the trouble to grab him as he left and try a little persuasion in the cellar of the rue Lauriston. Not that the brute had any evidence that he had crossed the demarcation line illegally, but just for the fun of watching him sweat.

The glass empty, Charles dropped some money on the table and strolled towards the door. There was a knot in the pit of his stomach that would not go away. As he passed the end of the bar, the bartender looked up and gave him a friendly nod. Charles waved his hand casually and hesitated. He was afraid, terribly afraid. His knees were weak, and there was a painful pounding in his head that almost blinded him. For a split second, he thought of asking Labru for help, but he fought down the impulse. The Café Denis was both a letter-drop and a "safe house" where messages were passed and endangered comrades hidden. With Blondie so close on his tail, he would be endangering the whole setup if he ran to the burly man for help. As he opened the door and left, the bartender looked after him pensively.

Outside the café, the dark street was empty. *They didn't have to watch too long,* Charles thought bitterly. *They know where I live.*

This time, he spent only three days in the "ice box," the enforced isolation of someone being watched by the enemy. One of Lafont's men had decided to hedge his bet on the outcome of the war by slipping information to the Resistance. He reported that Blondie had mentioned seeing Marceau at the Gare d'Austerlitz with his pretty

116

housemaid. Lafont had made a few lewd comments on what camping trips were for, and that had brought a lot of dutiful laughter. Then the whole thing had been forgotten in the planning of a new series of raids ordered by the Germans. There were rumors of a big push to neutralize the Resistance in the Paris area.

Vidal passed the word that all precautions were to be doubled and all contacts with other groups were to be held to a minimum. No one was to come to the printing shop unless directly ordered to do so. Necessary meetings would be made according to a schedule and at places that had been worked out long ago. The underground newspaper was now being printed in three separate places and stored in garages, warehouses, and apartments all over Paris. "Absolute discipline," the scar-faced man warned. "Remember, all they have to do is find one link in the chain and they roll up all of us."

On the morning of his third day in the "ice box," Charles was sitting at his desk writing a column for the newspaper. He had once complained to Kléber that the journalism and thinking in the paper were so poor that not only would it fail to convince and move the critical French, but it did not even justify the risks they took to distribute it under the noses of the Boches. "Do better," had been the old man's grumbling answer.

Now that he had the leisure, Charles had written a long analysis of why the clandestine struggle was so vital to France, why they owed it to the two million French soldiers in German prison camps to keep the flame of resistance burning so that it could never be said that France had been liberated from across the seas. "Our fathers, our uncles, and our brothers are behind barbed wire under enemy guns. Our fathers and our grandfathers brought us honor in the great victory of 1918, but now it is our turn to fight," he wrote. "One does not inherit his father's honor as one does his money. Every generation must struggle for it and if need be die for it. This is the privilege and duty of free men."

The ring of the telephone startled him as he was admiring his words. He waited for the third ring, then picked up the receiver. "Hello?"

The voice at the other end was muffled, as if someone was talking through a handkerchief. "Etoile 98–06?"

"You have the wrong number," Charles said curtly; then he listened carefully. There was a slight cough, then a click, and the connection was broken.

He went to the bookcase and found the street map of Paris. The code was a very simple one. The first letter of "Etoile" was E; the first number was nine. Locating "E-9" on the grid lines of the cross-hatched map, Charles put his finger on the Auteuil racetrack in the Bois de Boulogne—the south end near the Auteuil subway stop. He had been ordered to be there at 8:06 the next day.

When he arrived at the rendezvous, Vidal was standing near the main gate earnestly perusing a racing sheet. Charles smiled at the loud checked jacket that the serious Resistance leader was wearing, and at the ever-present blue tie with its anchor design. Vidal played the game to the hilt, angrily making check marks next to his selections and glancing up at the board that showed the late changes in the day's entries. He shook hands solemnly with Charles and they started to walk down the path past the stables.

"We're dispersing until we find out what this latest series of roundups means," the scar-faced man muttered. "You will take over all activities in the area south of the river. You know our man there. He'll give you all the names and hiding places, and you can work out a new schedule with him in the next two days. After that, he has another assignment, and you're on your own."

Charles flushed with pride and nodded. This was a big responsibility Vidal was giving him. Over thirty *résistants* would be under his orders. He tried to protest that he was not ready for such an important assignment, but Vidal cut him short with a wave of the hand. "Look, Falcon, you've been in the business over fifteen months now and you're still alive. That makes you a veteran. A lot of the people you will command are raw recruits. You'll have to train them, watch them, inspire them, and calm their fears—wet-nurse them the way we wet-nursed you. They will treat you with great respect, for Falcon is a name that is known and admired, but try not to let it go to your head."

"What about Blondie?"

"We're convinced that no more will come of that unfortunate encounter. Actually, he was at the station to check on a suspected arms shipment and just happened to spot you getting off the train."

"But he saw Majo when—" Even as the words sprang from his mouth, Charles realized his blunder.

Vidal's eyes narrowed and his thin lips tightened. They walked in silence for a moment, each locked in his own thoughts.

"All right," Vidal finally said. "I will overlook this one violation of discipline. I suppose it was inevitable that you learn her name—"

"In case the Boches should ask me," Charles said stubbornly.

"—on a mission such as that, but watch yourself. I'll be looking over your shoulder while you are operating down there south of the river, but I'm counting on you. Be careful in everything you do—especially security." The scar-faced man quickly took the racing sheet from his pocket and pointed to a name. "What do you think of Héloise in the third race?"

Charles saw the German officer approaching them a split second later. "A real dog," he said loudly. "Look what she did in the last two races . . . nothing at all."

The German major stared contemptuously at the two "gamblers" as he strode past. Charles could almost read the Fritz's thoughts: *The world is at war, France is occupied and humbled, and these two stand here worrying about horse races.*

As they walked back along the path, Vidal said quietly, "We have had quite a bit of radio traffic with London lately. Early this morning we got a message that your parents are well and safe in

England. Your father is serving with the Free French forces there."

Tears of gratitude filled Charles' eyes as he stammered his thanks. The flood of relief that filled him did not make him forget what this violation in radio discipline must have cost the strict Resistance leader. Vidal waved off his thanks and left, again reading his racing form.

That same afternoon Charles reported to a little jewelry shop in the university district and began his work. He was determined to succeed, if only to thank Vidal for his comradely gesture. Studying the list of storage places and the distribution schedule, he suddenly realized that today was his seventeenth birthday.

For the next month, Charles worked day and night, often sleeping in an army cot in the back of the store. He watched his people carefully and was satisfied with all but two: a man who drank and talked too much, and a hysterical woman who could not control her nerves. The woman he sent home politely, but the man had to be threatened, to make certain that he would fear the Resistance more than the Fritzes. "Get out and don't come near us again," Charles told him late one night. "If one indiscreet word escapes your lips—drunk or sober—one of us will be around to put an end to your babbling—forever." Pale as a ghost, the man had fled, and had not stopped running until he had reached Lille.

As Vidal had predicted, Falcon was shown great deference by the new recruits in the group. They were impressed by his youth, his long service in the Resistance, and his escape from the rue Lauriston. He overheard some whispers about his sorties across the demarcation line, and some hints that he had shot five German officers with his own hand. As often as he tried to deflate these romantic ideas, the myths persisted—even in men and women old enough to be his parents. They hung on his words during the training sessions and questioned nothing.

"Mind you, their discipline is good," he complained to Vidal at one of their rare meetings, "but for the wrong reasons. They haven't grasped that survival is also part luck, that what we do really is like playing Russian roulette. The odds are five to one that the trigger of the revolver will only click harmlessly, but one day, the single bullet will be under the firing pin and the game will be over."

Vidal refused to be shaken. "All you're telling me is that they look up to you as a model, a leader. That is very good. Incidentally, I knew about that drunken loudmouth, but I wanted to see how you would handle it, so I had him kept under observation until you took over and got rid of him. I know—it was a risk, but I had to see if you could do this job, and now I'm satisfied. Besides, you're not the only one with problems. We lost another distributor yesterday . . . a young girl caught with a bundle of newspapers coming out of the Levallois post office."

He saw Charles' face blanch and added hurriedly, "She was a new girl whom we called Sparrow. The parcel dropped and broke open right under the nose of a policeman."

Charles felt his heart pounding again. He could have sworn that it had stopped for a moment. He knew that Vidal had sent Majo to work with Kléber at Clignancourt on the northern edge of the city. He also knew that this had been done to keep them apart. He missed her and worried about her constantly. Trying to keep the anger from his voice, he reviewed the new precautions he had taken, the tightened security and the changes in personnel.

"I can see that you have it under control here," said Vidal when Charles had finished. "I wish I could say as much for the rest of the groups. London is demanding more and more information, and we're stretched very thin. Also, we have to keep an eye on Pascal, who is very jittery from being cooped up all this time. We don't dare let him out on the streets as long as these roundups are going on. His papers won't stand a close check. The last time I was there, Gilbert was threatening to shoot him if he didn't stop whining. All in all, a bad situation."

Vidal paused and stared pensively at Charles. "You look very tired. Are you getting enough sleep? Never mind answering that, I know you aren't . . . none of us is these days. Well, here's an order: go home and relax this weekend, and don't go back to the jewelry shop until Monday." At Charles' impassioned objection that the work had to be watched closely, the scar-faced man repeated firmly, "That's an order. No one can work under this strain without a rest. Take it easy this weekend, and don't go patronizing the flea market at Clignancourt, either, for a glimpse of your little friend." Charles reddened under Vidal's amused glance. That was exactly what he had thought of first.

It was the same dream he had had on and off since the trip to Vichy, only now the windmill was gone and a barn stood in its place. Dressed only in a white slip, the girl was half hidden in a pile of hay in the middle of the pasture and was staring at him wildly. He still could not see her face clearly—Emma Bovary or Majo, he did not know. Two people came out of the barn and walked towards him, shouting and waving: his father and his mother, both angry and disapproving. He tried to explain to them what had happened, but his voice was lost in the terrible pounding, the hammering that seemed to rise from the ground.

With a start, he sat up in bed and listened. Someone was banging on the concierge's door and shouting, "Open up! Police!" Luckily, he had gotten into the habit of sleeping in most of his clothes, so in seconds he had put on his shoes and jacket and was running for his escape route.

The window went up silently on greased runners. He was out on the fire escape and tiptoeing up to the roof when they started beating on his door. By the time they had smashed it in, he had clambered over the edge of the roof and was making his way to the far side.

It was dark—the moon had set hours before—but Charles knew every step of the way. Two flat roofs with skylights, then a sharply peaked one that he traversed carefully on his hands and knees. The tiles of the sloping mansard that followed were cold and moist, and Charles cursed the wooden soles and heels of his shoes, which kept slipping and clattering alarmingly. He ran swiftly over the next three roofs, vaulting the low walls that separated them, and then he dropped softly onto the last—that of the Hôtel Bretagne—and crawled to the parapet that overlooked the street.

As he had suspected, a black Renault stood at the corner and two dark figures were investigating the alleyway. By this time the whole block was probably sealed off. Behind him, in the darkness, he could hear angry voices shouting to one another. He had closed the window behind him, but there was no way to lock it. Now they were searching the roofs. The fire escape to the street was out of the question now, and the roof of the Bretagne was bare of any hiding place.

Charles moved swiftly and silently to the fire door that led to the top floor of the hotel. When he had first rehearsed this escape, he had examined the door and noted that the inside bolt could be seen through a slight gap between the door and the frame. From the inside pocket of his jacket he took a piece of heavy wire; he twisted the end of it slightly and carefully worked it through the gap until it touched the bolt handle. The voices behind him were getting closer and his hands were beginning to sweat, but he concentrated on raising the handle and working it back. Twice the wire slipped off and once it caught in the slide itself, but slowly the well-oiled bolt slid from the catch. There, it was done! He opened the door just enough to squeeze his body through, shot the bolt, and collapsed on the cement steps.

Charles heard the pursuers climbing over the parapet onto the roof. Someone yelled a question, probably to the men in the alley. There was a banging on the entry door behind which Charles was crouched, and a light blazed through the gap. Charles recognized Blondie's voice shouting orders. "Go back to the apartment and call the boss. Tell him that Marceau has given us the slip. Tell him that we're on our way to the avenue de Wagram. Then stay in the apartment in case that little rat returns."

There was a confusion of sounds on the roof, muffled voices, the clatter of heels on the fire escape; then silence. A car started up and tires squealed. Someone tried the door again and Charles cringed, pressing back against the wall. Then they were gone.

Charles sat limply trying to control his breathing. *Fear is normal,* he told himself, *panic is not.* He looked at the luminescent dial of his watch: 0337—an hour and a half until the curfew was over. Even then it would not be safe on the streets. He had to warn the others, but how? He could hardly saunter down into the lobby, ask the desk clerk for a token for the telephone . . . not without the police being called. And he couldn't stay hidden in the stairwell. Any minute now, the night watchman might be coming up to investigate the noise or to sneak a forbidden smoke. There was only one other way to get to a telephone—still risky, but if he was lucky, it just might work.

He felt his way cautiously down the cement steps, pushed the door at the bottom open a crack, and peered into the hallway. The Hôtel Bretagne was not "de luxe": worn carpet, walls and ceiling of a particularly hideous pink, all illuminated by a single bare bulb near the staircase. Charles listened at the nearest door. Someone laughed loudly inside; no good, he wanted someone already asleep. Outside the next door, a pair of men's black pumps and a pretty pair of evening slippers stood side by side. *That's it,* Charles thought. *With a woman in the room, he's not likely to try something heroic.* He rapped on the door.

"Who is it?" a sleepy, irritated voice demanded.

"Telegram, monsieur."

There was a muffled conversation, the sound of footsteps, the snap of a light switch, and the sound of a bolt being withdrawn. As soon as the door started to open, Charles hit it with his shoulder, pushed his way into the room, and slammed the door behind him.

From his sitting position on the floor where the door had flung him, the gray-haired man stared, his mouth open. The woman, younger and almost pretty, clutched the bedclothes to her chest in fright. They both had their eyes fixed on Charles' hand hidden in his jacket pocket, which bulged ominously. The man was making a strange clicking sound as he tried to protest.

"Be quiet," Charles said menacingly. "You are in no danger if you do exactly as I say. Don't try anything stupid. This is Resistance business, understand?"

The man nodded foolishly and stopped clicking. The woman bit on the top of the sheet to keep from crying out.

"All right, both of you, into the bathroom and shut the door." Charles glanced into the bathroom to make certain there was no exit or telephone there, helped the man off the floor, and pushed him none too gently after the woman. Before closing the door, he asked, "What's your name?"

"Lebon, Etienne. I'm a lawyer from Soissons," was the frightened reply. The woman said nothing and Charles made a bet with himself that her name was not Lebon.

The telephone was on the night table next to the bed. Charles sat wearily on the edge of the bed and lifted the receiver. The desk clerk took a long time to wake up and answer. "Hello?"

"This is Monsieur Lebon in room 41. Please get me Élysées 74–22." There was a mutter about people who made telephone calls in the middle of the night; then Charles heard the phone ringing in the printing shop. It rang once, and then someone answered, "Printing shop."

Charles slammed down the receiver and buried his head in his hands. If all had been well at the shop, the telephone would have been allowed to ring four times and the answer would have been "Élysées 73–22"—one digit off.

The Gestapo had taken the printing shop and probably everyone in it.

When the trembling had stopped, he picked up the phone again and apologetically asked for another number. This time it rang a long time before it was answered. There was the sound of voices and some blaring music in the background.

"Café Denis. Labru speaking."

"Falcon." There was a pause as the burly bartender carried the phone into the back room.

"Where are you?"

"Hôtel Bretagne, rue Copernic. Room 41."

"Listen carefully. All hell has broken loose. Stay under cover there. At exactly 6:20, a blue paneled delivery truck will pull up in front of the hotel. The driver will be wearing sunglasses." There was a click as Labru hung up.

Charles made one more call. This time the phone rang the correct number of times before someone picked it up, and the code answer was right. Charles repeated one word—"Alarm!"—twice, heard the confirmation that it was understood, and returned the receiver to its cradle. At least all was well south of the river.

He knocked politely on the bathroom door and invited the couple to join him. If he left them in there too long, one or the other might have hysterics and start screaming. Better to have them out where he could watch them. It was going to be a long three hours.

All he could think of was Majo in Clignancourt. What had happened up there? Labru was a veteran and unflappable. If he called it all hell breaking loose, then it was very bad indeed.

The thought of the cellar and the hideous bleeding figure made him tremble again.

8

"Please sit down, Falcon," the fat man said, indicating a chair on the opposite side of the long table. He opened a manila folder and was soon deep in a study of its contents, occasionally pushing the gold-rimmed glasses back on the bridge of his fleshy nose. Charles sank gratefully into the well-upholstered chair and looked around the room.

Six hours earlier, he had sauntered through the lobby of the Hôtel Bretagne, nodded to the room clerk, and walked out into the bright sunlight. The blue truck had been standing at the curb, the driver feeding charcoal into the boiler strapped to the fender. As soon as Charles had jumped into the back, the driver had locked the rear doors and had driven off.

It had been a long trip with many stops in the early morning traffic. From the sounds—the whistles of barges on the river, the banging of trains in a freight yard, the cries of peddlers in a market—he had been able to guess that they had been somewhere in the northeast suburbs. He had thought he recognized the bells of the Church of Sacré Coeur as they'd passed through Montmartre, and the laboring of the *gazogène* had indicated that they were climbing some fairly steep hills. The truck had stopped finally and there had been the sound of muffled voices. A few minutes later, the back doors had been unlocked and the driver, still wearing sunglasses, had handed him a bag and a blanket. There had been no conversation and no hint as to where he was being taken. Wrapping himself in the blanket against the cold, Charles had munched half-heartedly at the bread and cheese, and had taken a few swallows of the cheap wine that had been in the bag.

The hours had passed slowly. Inside the cold stuffy van, Charles had drowsed on and off, fighting against the fear that threatened to grip him. That the network had been "taken" he knew, but who had been arrested? The uncertainty about the fate of his companions had been the worst fear of all. It had twisted his stomach and made his head swim. Majo, Vidal, old Kléber . . . where were they?

The motor had started and the truck had jolted forward, throwing him against the floor. He had looked at his watch: noon. *Lebon and his girlfriend are probably sitting down to a good lunch*, he had thought mirthlessly. After all, they had been up early and couldn't have had much appetite for breakfast.

This time the trip had been short, only ten minutes. The doors had opened and Labru had been standing next to the driver. Charles had clambered out and been hustled into a red brick warehouse. He had caught a hasty glimpse of a factory, a garage, and the stark ironwork of a power plant not far off. Belleville, he had guessed. The "Red Quarter" of Paris.

They had walked past two young men lounging nonchalantly inside the warehouse door, then down a long corridor and up a flight of steps. The office had been at the back of the second floor, guarded by still another young man who had smiled politely as they'd passed. There had been a gun stuck in the belt under his half-opened windbreaker.

The fat man had been sitting behind the desk, telephoning, when Charles and Labru had entered, leaving the driver talking to the guard. It had not been a long conversation, but Charles had caught a few words: "Pantin . . . yes, I see. . . . The garage . . . how many? . . . Very well, we'll let you know." Then he had hung up, wiped his hands fastidiously with a handkerchief, risen from behind the desk, and come forward to greet them.

I know him, Charles had thought. *I've seen that short dumpy figure, that brush mustache, that bow tie. . . . Of course! He was a deputy in the National Assembly before the war, Secretary of the French Communist Party—his picture was in the newspapers often. When the party was declared illegal at the outbreak of the war, he went underground. Rumor had it that he and he alone had decided on the assassination of German officers. What was his name—Durand, Dufour . . . no, Duclos. Jacques Duclos.*

Labru, silent and deferential, and Charles sat on one side of the conference table while Duclos, seated opposite them, went through the folder. In the corner, a young woman in a flowered blouse sat primly behind a typewriter waiting for instructions. *It could be a business office anywhere in Paris—the boss, his secretary, Labru the foreman, and the rebellious employee about to be sacked,* Charles thought bitterly. *Why the hell doesn't he begin?*

Duclos shut the folder and looked up at the boy. "This is an inquiry into the fate of the Vidal-Kléber network, ordered by the Central Committee to determine what happened and whether it represents an immediate danger to us. I assure you, Falcon, we only want to help . . . if we can. Here are the facts as we now know them."

Adjusting his glasses, the fat man cleared his throat and began to read from the folder. "Last month—October 9, 1941—Gilbert and Pascal arrived from London to set up a radio for the Vidal-Kléber group. Communication with London was established, allowing the transmittal of intelligence and the reception of messages about arms drops and the arrival of other agents. . . ."

The soft voice droned on and on, detailing the military information that had been gathered, the arms received, money, propaganda material—even the code names of the agents, their arrival times, and their present locations. *They know a lot about us,* Charles thought. *The Communists must spend as much time and energy spying on the non-Communist Resistance as they do fighting the Fritzes. Why does he go on like this? Why doesn't he tell me what happened to Majo and the others?*

Even Labru was beginning to twist uneasily in

his chair as the lecture went on in monotonous detail about the setup in the apartment above the garage and the security measures taken to protect the radio. Suddenly, Charles' irritation vanished and he sat bolt upright to listen.

"The radio operator known as Pascal was incapable of the discipline that his necessarily enforced isolation called for. On the night of November 17—that is, last night—he slipped out of the garage and went to a black-market night club called the White Peacock on the rue d'Artois. Evidently he was known there, for the owner—one Cassoulles, called the Strong Man—greeted him by name and supplied him with whiskey and one of the girls. Two hours after his arrival, four French Gestapo agents came into the club, spoke briefly with the Strong Man, and arrested Pascal. They took him to 93 rue Lauriston, where he was seen struggling and protesting as he was dragged inside."

Duclos paused and said apologetically, "Unfortunately, our man inside the rue Lauriston—" *The same double agent,* Charles thought, *playing both sides of the street—*"was not present when Pascal arrived, so we are not certain of the exact details of the interrogation. However, we can guess from what happened one hour later."

He adjusted the gold-rimmed glasses and continued reading. "Shortly after 3 A.M., four cars carrying Lafont's men left the rue Lauriston. One group surrounded the printing shop and arrested Vidal, Raven, Dove, Fox, and Beaver. The second group took the radio operator, Pascal, to the garage. They overpowered the guard, but the English agent Gilbert had heard them coming and opened fire. He succeeded in killing one Gestapo man and wounding another, but finally was trapped in the back room and killed by a machine-gun burst. He had destroyed the radio and burnt the codes before falling.

"The third group went to the apartment house at 17 rue Copernic where Falcon lived. They broke down the door, but Falcon had escaped over the roof. He is now assisting in this inquiry. The last group raided the Restaurant Seville in Clignancourt . . ."

It was like a blow in the stomach. Charles doubled up with pain. There was a loud buzzing in his ears and Duclos' words seemed to be coming from a great distance away. He felt Labru's hand grasp his shoulder sympathetically.

". . . and arrested everyone on the premises. In the cellar, they found large numbers of a clandestine newspaper. Among those handcuffed and taken away were Kléber, Tiger, and Seagull."

The fat man coughed and waved Labru away from Charles.

"You can appreciate the problem, Falcon. The radio operator has been 'turned.' He's now working for Lafont. So far, he has only been able to give the names and places he knows, but soon they'll be driving him around Paris and he'll spot a familiar face, someone he only saw at a distance, someone who only came to the garage once. And even more dangerous is the fact that the Germans can make him reestablish radio contact with London. Every agent parachuted into

France, every arms shipment, will fall into their hands."

"But the radio was destroyed," Charles blurted, "the codes burnt. Gilbert gave his life for that."

Duclos shook his head. "That was useless. Pascal knows the frequencies, the codes, and the time schedules. He can use any radio. The important thing is his 'fist,' the rhythm with which he transmits. That, and the false words he puts in at certain points in the message to show that it is genuine and that he does not have a German pistol at his head."

Labru cursed under his breath while the fat man made a notation in the folder. "If your friends in London had trusted us enough to send us a radio too, we could let them know about Pascal," Duclos complained. "As it is, there is only one way to prevent him from doing more damage with his treason."

From the beginning, Charles had understood that the radio operator must die. What concerned him now was not an ethical but a tactical question: how—and when. The Gestapo was certain to keep a close guard on its prize prisoner. It would not be easy.

"There's no chance of getting him when he's taken from Gestapo headquarters on the avenue Foch back to Lafont's place," Labru said. "We'll never get word in time. We could attack the rue Lauriston when we know he's there and—"

"Forget it," Charles interrupted. "The place is a fortress. There are too many men inside armed with submachine guns. You'd have to fight your way through a dozen rooms, blowing open oak

doors, to get to Pascal. They have an alarm system to the German barracks less than a mile
away, so you'd be attacked from the rear in seven
or eight minutes. No, it can't be done by force. it
will have to be one man, silently, swiftly."

Duclos nodded his agreement and pressed a
button on the desk. "We have such a man available. He has some experience in these matters."

Charles turned as the office door opened. The
fat man and Labru were watching him closely.

Lynx walked into the room.

But Charles was beyond shock, and his expression did not change. When he spoke, his voice
was calm and steady, but held an underlying
thread of contempt.

"I don't think you'll get close enough to Pascal
to be able to shoot him in the back at point-blank
range. I'm the only one who has seen and spoken
to Pascal, so there will be no possibility of a mistake. Also, I have been inside the house in the rue
Lauriston. I know the layout."

"Labru will supply you with whatever you
need," Duclos said promptly, "including guards to
cover your escape. Provision will be made to get
you to the Spanish border afterwards." It was
clear from his tone that they were dismissed, that,
a decision having been made in this troublesome
affair, he had lost interest in it.

Charles rose slowly from the chair, then leaned
over the desk and said, "Incidentally, Duclos
. . ." The fat man stiffened at the use of his
name. Clearly he thought Charles had overstepped
himself. "Let's get one thing very clear. This
is not a suicide mission. I fully intend to kill Pas-

cal and get out of Paris in one piece. If those guards aren't there to cover my retreat, my people will know about it. Sooner or later, London will know of it, and it will go very hard with you indeed." He felt Labru pulling him away, but he was determined to wipe the smug, satisfied smile off the fat man's face. "Don't think that the Fritzes got all of us. After I called Labru, I made another call and alerted my people south of the river. Right now they are in hiding, but they will be very interested in what happens to me."

Opening the folder, Duclos penciled a notation. "The jewelry store on the Boulevard Saint-Michel? I believe Eagle, the cab driver, is your second-in-command? You can send him a postcard from Spain. Now, if you're ready, Labru will show you our arsenal."

As Charles left the room without a look at Lynx, the fat man stared pensively at his back.

The "arsenal" was laid out on a bare plank in a deep cellar beneath the warehouse. It was an astonishing display of revolvers, automatic pistols, rifles of every size and caliber, grenades, two sawed-off shotguns, even knives and knuckle dusters. Charles picked a gun at random and inspected the breech and bore. It was spotless and well-oiled. He knew about guns, both from his hunting trips with his father and from practice on a firing range. He had never seen such a weird assortment of weapons. "Where did you get these?" he asked Labru.

The bartender grinned with pride. "From the sewers, mostly. Before the war, whenever some tough guy was on the run from the police after a robbery, he'd slide his gun down into the sewers. It was worth five years more in jail if he was caught with it, you know. Well, the sewer workers are good comrades and party members. When they found one of these in time, before it got too rusty or beat up, they turned it over to us. Our people cleaned and repaired it, and we stored it away for the future."

To use against the government in a revolution, Charles thought. *They never guessed they would be using them to kill Nazi officers in Paris.*

"What about ammunition?"

"At least ten rounds for every weapon, more for the rifles and the Schmeisser submachine gun."

"Recent manufacture?" Labru nodded appreciatively at the question. Charles knew that old ammunition had a tendency to misfire because the primers deteriorated, and on a job like this, that would be an unacceptable risk.

"Pick your weapon and we'll give you bullets made less than six months ago," the bartender boasted.

Charles stared thoughtfully at the arms spread out haphazardly on the unpainted plank. No rifles or submachine guns . . . too hard to conceal; automatic pistols had an unfortunate habit of jamming when fired rapidly; knives were ridiculous and grenades uncertain. The shotgun was possible, but the recoil was certain to throw his aim off. No, it had to be a pistol with an easy trigger pull and a long barrel for accuracy.

Most of the pistols he immediately rejected as being too light or having too small a caliber, too short a barrel, or some slight pitting in the bore that would affect the bullet's trajectory in an un-predictable manner. He picked up a Smith and Wesson .38 and hefted it expertly. Good solid feel and nice balance. He squeezed the trigger, snapped out the cylinder, sighted through the bore, and ran his finger inside the breech. It was clean except for a slight film of oil. Perfect.

The bartender brought him a box of cartridges with a recent date stamped on it. Charles examined the cartridges carefully and selected twelve. He set these aside and dumped the rest of the box into his jacket pocket. "Can I practice down here?" he asked.

"You're thirty feet below the street," Labru said. "No one will hear."

They set up a narrow plank against the earth wall at the back of the cellar. There was a large brown knot in it at the level of a man's chest. Charles paced off forty-five feet and made a mark on the floor. That would be the distance across Lafont's office from the balcony window to the door. He loaded the gun with six of the extra cartridges and began to fire at the brown knot. First slow fire with careful aim between each shot; then rapid bursts of three. After each six shots, he inspected the target and drew penciled circles around the points of impact. Finally he was satisfied and asked for a cleaning kit.

The explosions in the closed-off cellar had been painful to the ears, but Charles welcomed the pain. It helped to wipe out the picture that had filled his mind since he had learned the truth—the image of Majo's soft white throat and Engel's brutal hairy hands. Now there was nothing to think about except the job to be done. He would kill the radio operator because it was what she and the others would expect him to do. It would not save them, but they would know that the Resistance continued, and that their agony was not in vain.

Majo, I can't help you. I love you and I can't save you. Forgive me.

This time they used a moving van and parked it around the corner from the rue Lauriston. There was someone in the Café Normandy waiting for the telephone call that would tell them that Pascal had arrived for his last meeting with Lafont.

Hidden behind some large crates in the back of the van, Charles and Labru sat quietly in the darkness waiting for the signal. They had reviewed the plan for the last time and now there was nothing more to say. As the minutes passed, the bartender twisted about nervously, rubbing his hands against the cold. In forty minutes the curfew would begin, and some curious policeman would start wondering about an apparently abandoned moving van.

Charles heard Labru beating his hands against his shoulders to keep his circulation going. He himself had dressed against the cold: heavy slacks and shirt, a sweater and a windbreaker, all in dark colors difficult to spot at night. He could feel the gun shoved into his belt. His mind was empty, but he was annoyed at his companion's nervousness.

"Sit still, Labru," he said. "They can hear your heart pounding a mile away."

With a sigh of embarrassment, the bartender

141

relaxed and stared up into the dark. "Falcon?" Charles did not answer. "What you said to Duclos . . . I want you to know that the guards are there. I give you my word on it."

Charles grunted and, taking the extra gun clip from his pocket, ran his fingers over it again. The six bullets mounted in a steel ring would enable him to reload quickly once the spent cases were rejected. Not that he thought there would be time, but one never knew.

"Well, anyway," the bartender continued hoarsely, "I wanted you to know . . . no matter what happens . . . I think you are one helluva man."

The rapping on the side of the van startled them. Two short—pause—then two more. It was the signal. Pascal had entered the house on the rue Lauriston.

The rear door was unlocked by someone outside. They waited for the knock that would indicate that the street was clear. Charles zipped up his windbreaker, turned, and offered his hand to Labru. It was seized in a firm grip and pumped vigorously. *He doesn't expect me to make it,* Charles thought. *Well, he's wrong.*

At the first rap on the door, he pushed it open and jumped into the street. The driver had parked so that the rear was opposite the alleyway, and, after a quick glance around, Charles walked into the dark alley. As he groped his way along the narrow path between the two walls, he heard the truck start up and drive off.

They had gone over the route several times with one of Labru's men, who had paced it off. Exactly forty-two paces down the alley filled with garbage cans and boxes of refuse there would be a door with a chalked cross on it. Normally it would be locked, but Labru's man guaranteed that tonight it would be unbolted. "It had better be," the burly bartender had growled. This door led into the basement of the apartment house next to Lafont's headquarters. Across the basement was a metal fire door that opened on a flight of stairs leading to the ground floor and then up three stories to the roof. Turning left on the roof, one came to the parapet and could look down on the balcony that ran around three sides of Number 93. There were three windows and a door off the balcony and, below it, an interior garden surrounded by a high wall with a bolted gate leading to the back street. There was a guard with a submachine gun sitting in a chair inside the gate. He was relieved every four hours.

The hinges of the marked door had been oiled and it opened quietly. Swiftly, Charles crossed the basement, opened the fire door, and raced up the four flights to the roof. On his hands and knees, he made his way to the parapet and cautiously looked down.

It was exactly as described: the balcony, windows, door; and in the darkness he could make out the form of the guard seated near the garden gate. He made his way along the parapet until he was out of the guard's line of vision and then slid carefully over the wall and let himself dangle until his swinging feet caught the railing of the balcony. Pushing himself with all his strength away from the wall, he dropped lightly onto the metal grating of the balcony and lay there listening.

There was no sound of alarm. After taking a moment to catch his breath, he pulled himself towards the street side of the house.

As he had expected, the steel shutters were closed, but through a slight gap he could see about half of each room. Through the first window, he saw four men playing cards. They were talking in low voices. Lounging against the door, Blondie was cleaning his fingernails with a knife and commenting on the game.

The next window was Lafont's office, and Charles felt a cold chill as he recognized the desk and the chair. The room was empty. He slid along the wall to the third window and peered through the crack in the shutters. At first he thought this room was also vacant, but even as the pang of disappointment tore through him, a man walked into view.

All Charles could see was the back of a black uniform with silver braid on the sleeves, a broad black belt and holster, and a shiny ceremonial dagger at the left. A Gestapo officer, he thought.

"I can assure you, my dear Vogtler, that the man is with us one hundred percent." The high-pitched voice came from somewhere behind the right shutter. Charles froze and gripped the revolver in his belt. Lafont!

The officer stopped and blew a cloud of cigarette smoke towards the ceiling. "We must be absolutely certain of him, M. Henri. If he fails to put in the security words—and we will have only his word for it—this whole radio game can turn into a disaster for us."

"But surely when the English agents arrive on schedule—" the falsetto voice protested.

"Na, na. The damned British are old hands at this business. They are quite capable of deliberately sending us agents loaded with false information that the spies themselves believe to be true. Then when we act on it, say to protect the submarine pens at Brest, the R.A.F. strikes elsewhere."

Lafont swore mightily at the duplicity of the Anglo-Americans. To sacrifice their own people . . . even in war there had to be some decency.

"Let's have Pascal in once more," Vogtler said. "I want to know more about the radio training methods at that spy school."

As Lafont picked up the telephone, Charles took out his knife and carefully lifted the shutter bar off the latch. It was a surprisingly simple lock, for the French Gestapo agents had never dreamed of any threat but a burst of gunfire from a passing car. Charles took the revolver from his belt and slid off the safety. His mouth was dry and he could hear the blood pounding in his ears, but he glanced down and saw that his hand was steady. Well, almost. . . . As desperately as he wanted to see the door, he did not dare push on the opened shutter in case it should creak.

It could not have been more than two minutes, but it seemed like hours to the boy crouched on the balcony. Finally Pascal fell into the room, pushed by a sneering Engel. As the German officer moved, Charles could see the sweating radio man collapsed in a chair near the center of the room.

145

Blondie stood behind him as Pascal looked anxiously from Lafont to Vogtler.

Thirty feet, Charles thought coldly. *Maybe thirty-two—no more.*

Ignoring the radio operator's protests—"I've cooperated with you at the risk of my life"—Vogtler began to question him.

"What are the false words you put in your radio messages to indicate that you are free?"

"I told you," Pascal bleated.

Lafont laughed contemptuously at his terror. "Tell me again," the officer demanded.

"The message is in groups of five. Every fifth group has the second—"

Now! Charles shoved the shutter open and pulled the trigger rapidly three times.

Labru accelerated quickly and the car leaped forward up the hill. "Go on." he growled.

Slumped in the seat next to him, Charles stared out the window at the blurred shops flying by and tried to remember what had happened. "My first three shots were too fast, but I was lucky. One hit Pascal high in the shoulder and lifted him out of the chair. He was terrified. He didn't know where the shooting was coming from, so he turned toward the only exit he saw—the window! I aimed the next two shots and saw them hit him in the chest. The German, Vogtler, had his gun out, so I gave him the last shot. I think I hit him in the face. At least I have an impression of a bright red mask suddenly covering it."

Charles pressed his feverish head against the cold window and fought the nausea and weakness

146

that filled him. "I don't remember anything after that."

"What about Lafont and Engel?"

"The shutter protected Lafont, and Blondie hit the floor at the first shot. There was no time to reload."

Labru shook his head in admiration. "Twenty-six minutes from the time you left the van until you reached the car at the other end of the alley. Not bad, Falcon, not bad at all."

They drove in silence for a while. Charles saw two policemen stop and stare at the speeding car. *I don't care,* he thought dully. *I just don't care.* It was not Pascal that bothered him—Charles had prepared himself for what he'd had to do—but the horrible sight of Vogtler's face haunted him. That scarlet death's mask . . . even if he was the enemy . . .

"Give me the gun," the bartender said quietly. Charles took it from his belt and handed it over. Labru shoved it into the glove compartment under some rags. "In an hour," he said, "the car and the gun will be at the bottom of the Seine. We're keeping you in a 'safe house' tonight, and tomorrow morning you leave for Spain."

"Labru," Charles pleaded, "is there any hope for my friends?"

"I'm sorry, Falcon, none. They're in the prison at Fresnes all right, in separate cells, closely guarded. We can't get near them. They're being interrogated at night, all through the night. As far as we know, no one has broken."

Dove, Charles suddenly remembered—that was the gray-haired woman, in the classroom, the one who was always so afraid. Beaver was only fifteen, always joking. He tried to picture Fox, but couldn't single out his face.

No one had broken—the ultimate accolade.

"Goodbye," he whispered. Goodbye to Vidal in that checkered coat, playing the racing tout; goodbye to wonderful old Kléber, who yelled and screamed at them and had made them soldiers in this underground war; goodbye to Majo. . . . The tears came unbidden to his eyes and he turned his face away to mourn alone for his comrades.

Labru whipped the car around a corner and settled down to the last run. He glanced over at the boy huddled against the car door, his shoulders shaking. Without taking his eyes off the road, he reached over, gripped Charles' arm, and squeezed affectionately.

"As I said, Falcon, one helluva man."

9

The beach was a dirty yellow ribbon that stretched as far as the eye could see. Long twisted coils of rusty barbed wire embroidered its edge, and here and there faded white signs warned of minefields. A chill wind whipped up the sand and dotted the waters of the Channel with whitecaps, sweeping them in from the distant hazy blur that was the horizon. Here on the south coast of England, the threat of a German invasion was long gone, but the signs of British defiance remained.

Charles and his mother walked along the pebbled road that paralleled the shore. Most of the time they were silent, troubled that in twenty months they had become strangers. Their meeting in the hotel had been warm and emotional, but soon they had stepped back embarrassed, as if they had made a mistake in recognition.

He's taller, his mother noted, *and heavier, and there's that wild, hunted look in his eyes. Even as he talks, he keeps looking over his shoulder to see if anyone is close enough to hear. When we passed that woman walking her dog along the path, he was silent and turned to make certain that she did not follow us. He was such a loving child, always in my arms—my* Beau Sabreur. *Now there is a wall between us. Oh, he is polite enough in a formal way, but he seems to be looking past me, perhaps to find those he left behind.* She held his arm tighter, as if afraid that he would suddenly run away.

Aware of his mother's anguish, Charles tried to pick up the thread of the story once more. It was still painful to talk about it, but he felt an obligation—as if he had to explain his absence like a truant. There were long pauses as he struggled to get the words past the tightness in his throat.

"They got me over the mountain trails into Spain in spite of the snow and the patrols, and I got as far as Pamplona before some Civil Guard asked for my papers. I spent two months in a filthy camp—flies, sand, crowded huts, and garbage for food—before the British consul got me released. He sent me to Lisbon, where eventually I got space on a tramp steamer that arrived in convoy at Portsmouth." He did not tell her that the steamer had been carrying high-octane gasoline and that the second night out two ships in the convoy had been torpedoed, one only two hundred yards away.

"When I landed, there were a Free French captain and two British military policemen waiting for me. They hustled me into a car and drove me to an interrogation center—I think it was near Reading. For five days they questioned me, Captain Lenoir and a British civilian named Lofting—all sorts of questions, but mostly they were interested in how the Fritzes had broken up our network. They became very suspicious when I

150

told them about Duclos and Labru, and I don't think they believed me when I told them how I killed Pascal and the Gestapo officer."

His mother gasped and turned her head away to hide the tears. Charles persisted in describing what had happened in the rue Lauriston. He wanted her to understand, to hear everything. "Oh yes, Maman, I killed them. Pascal was a traitor and a threat to all of us. The Nazi just got in the way."

He continued his story in a matter-of-fact voice.

"That was on the third day of the interrogation and they must have checked, because the next day they were much friendlier. They drove me to Free French Intelligence in London—I was relieved to see that the city was still standing, although I never believed the Nazi boasts—and I had to repeat the whole story again to a bunch of colonels. They wanted to know about the organization of the Communists in the Resistance, how many men, how well armed, what their plans were . . . stuff I had no idea of. I asked about Vidal and Kléber and . . . the others, but they mumbled and shuffled their papers and said they would try to find out.

"That night, Lofting came to my room, handed me a large piece of paper, and left without a word. I think I knew what it was even before unfolding it—it had a big black border. You see, Maman, the Fritzes like to advertise. They put up these execution notices all over Paris so people will know and be afraid."

In a choked, broken voice, he recited the words that were seared forever on his brain: "The following were condemned to death by a German military tribunal for espionage and acts of violence against the German army. They were shot this morning. Signed: von Stülpnagel, the German Military Commander in France."

Charles paused to take a deep breath before continuing. "There were nine names on the list, in alphabetical order. For the first time, I learned the real names and ages and occupations of my comrades." His mother shivered at the grief in his voice as he called off the list of the dead.

"Bruller, Marcel, twenty-two, student. That was Raven. His father was blinded by gas in the first war. The old man wanted to join him in the Resistance, but we had to say no.

"Chautemps, André-Louis, thirty-eight, naval officer. Vidal, the brains and heart of our group. He always wore the necktie of the Naval Academy. It was dangerous and silly, but very brave. Captain Lenoir told me that Vidal was badly burnt when his destroyer was bombed and sunk off Dunkirk.

"Fabre, Etienne, twenty-seven, metal worker. We called him Mammoth, he was so big and strong. He was in charge of sabotage in his factory.

"Laniel, René, sixty-two, no occupation. That was my wonderful old Kléber. I'll bet he told the Nazis what his occupation was, but they didn't dare print it: 'dedicated anti-Fascist' or 'French patriot.' That was his job and his life."

One by one, he tolled off the names of his dead comrades, refusing to let them disappear into their graves without this last tribute, this last prayer.

When he was done, he answered the question in his mother's eyes. "They shot only the men. The two women, Seagull and Dove, were sentenced to twenty years in the concentration camp at Ravensbrück. That, too, is a death sentence, for no one leaves that camp alive."

At the pier, they turned and walked back with the wind behind them. *My son, my son,* Mme. Marceau grieved silently. *How can I ever reach you now with all these poor dead souls between us?*

"I had a letter from your father last week," she said timidly. "He is now a lieutenant-colonel and a liaison officer with the British headquarters in Cairo. I wired him last night that you were here with me safe at last."

Charles nodded indifferently. Before the war, his father's promotion would have been cause for great rejoicing, but now it seemed almost irrelevant. "What news is there from America now that they are in the war?" he asked soberly. The disaster at Pearl Harbor and the declaration of war by Germany and Italy on the United States had reached him through the Spanish newspapers in the internment camp. There had been consternation among the guards and joy among the French, Belgian, and Dutch internees.

"Your grandfather is in Washington trying to be useful. Your cousin Paul has joined the Air Force and is in training in Arizona." *Dropping bombs from ten thousand feet or machine-gunning trains from a safe altitude, that will be his war,* Charles thought disdainfully. *I wonder if he can shoot a man in the face at point-blank range and not throw up?* He remembered his American cousin as a chubby little boy who was a bit of a bully.

His mother spoke proudly of her relatives and of how the American people were now united in the war effort, how gasoline and food were soon to be rationed, how the factories were being converted to turn out planes and tanks, but Charles was not listening. A single seagull was circling above the sunlit waters and he watched it until it disappeared in the haze.

Majo, I love you.

". . . and they say the first American troops will be in England this month. Oh Charles, think how wonderful it will be to see our boys again."

"Not *my* boys, Maman. I'm French. The American part is an accident—a happy accident, but no more." He paused, then spoke the really difficult words. "Before I left London, I had another interview with Captain Lenoir. He says my experience with the Resistance in France is invaluable. I once mocked the idea of sixteen-year-old tank drivers, but now seventeen-year-old spies are indispensable. Well, anyway, I've enlisted in the Free French Intelligence Service. I'm to report to a training school in Wales in two weeks."

The stunned, shattered look on his mother's face filled him with remorse. He added quickly, "But we do have two weeks together, to talk stroll along this lovely beach with its ba and mines."

His weak attempt at humor fell flat. "Will they send you back to France?" his mother asked.

No point in lying, he thought miserably. *She may as well know the whole truth.* "Eventually, yes, but not for a long time. I'm not what you would call a trained agent yet. Besides, there will be lots of leaves. Perhaps Papa will come home—I mean to England—and we can spend some time together."

His mother shivered and wrapped her coat more tightly about her. "The wind is colder. I think I'll return to the hotel."

Charles nodded and watched her walk slowly up the path until she vanished behind the dunes. *Maman, I'm sorry to put more gray hairs on your head, but I must do this.*

Although she had not reproached him about his decision, he knew what it would mean for her to lose him again. He shrugged his shoulders fatalistically, thinking that his mother had now lost him twice: to the Resistance, and to a poor girl in that hell of Ravensbrück. There was no help for it. Majo had the greater claim to his love . . . and to his loyalty.

He wandered along the path, kicking at the pebbles and peering past the beach beyond the twisted wire with its cruel thorns, towards something lost in the blue-gray haze in the distance.

Words read by his old English master floated through his mind: "For I shall lay me down and bleed awhile/And then arise and fight again."

A seagull glided across the beach towards him, circled once, and then, rising high in the skies, flew swiftly towards France.

Postscript

This book is a fictional re-creation of the years of terror and courage when France was occupied by the German army. It is based on my narrative history of that grim period, *The French Against the French* (J.B. Lippincott Co., 1974), and while I have tried to be accurate and faithful to detail, the reader may want to know which characters are real and which are fictional.

There was a French Gestapo headquarters at 93 rue Lauriston headed by the ex-convict Henri Lafont, and Louis Engel was one of his henchmen. After the liberation of France in 1944, they were both executed by a French firing squad.

A German naval officer named Alphonse Moser was killed in the Barbès subway station and the Germans executed one hundred hostages in retaliation.

Jacques Bonsergent was the first Parisian shot by the Nazis for resistance.

English intelligence agents worked in many parts of occupied France, and at least one was captured and "turned" by the Gestapo.

Seventeen-year-old Guy Môquet was shot as a

hostage for the assassination of the German commandant of Nantes.

Jacques Duclos was indeed the head of the Communist Resistance.

And "Max" was the code name of Jean Moulin, who was captured and tortured to death by the Nazis in 1943. Today, he is buried in the Pantheon in Paris, mourned by a grateful nation.

M.D.

A Revealing Novel about Teenagers—
by a Teenager

THE OUTSIDERS

by S. E. Hinton

"The Outsiders," a rough and swinging gang of teen-agers from the wrong side of the tracks, have little hope for the material pleasures of American life. Their mode of expression is violence—directed toward the group of privileged kids who are at once objects of their envy and their hatred. "Written by a most perceptive teenager. It attempts to communicate to adults their doubts, their dreams, and their needs."—*Book Week*

A Laurel-Leaf Paperback $1.50

LAUREL-LEAF LIBRARY